COMING OUT OF THE COLD

A RAGS TO ROMANCE BOOK

MALLORY MONROE

**Visit
amazon.com/author/mallorymonroe
or
mallorymonroe.com
or
austinbrookpublishing.com**

**for more information on all of her
titles.**

**THE RAGS TO ROMANCE SERIES
STANDALONE BOOKS
IN PUBLICATION ORDER:**

WAITRESS
18. LOVE COMES FOR CHRISTMAS
19. LOVE AGAINST THE ODDS
20. DON'T LEAVE ME THIS WAY
21. JANARDI AND HIS MUSE
22. THE BILLIONAIRE AND HIS DRIVER
23. COMING OUT OF THE COLD

MALLORY MONROE SERIES:
THE RENO GABRINI/MOB BOSS SERIES (22 BOOKS)
THE SAL GABRINI SERIES (15 BOOKS)
THE TOMMY GABRINI SERIES (11 BOOKS)
THE MICK SINATRA SERIES (19 BOOKS)
THE BIG DADDY SINATRA SERIES (8 BOOKS)
THE TEDDY SINATRA SERIES (5 BOOKS)
THE TREVOR REESE SERIES (3 BOOKS)
THE AMELIA SINATRA SERIES (3 BOOKS)
THE BRENT SINATRA SERIES (2 BOOKS)

THE ALEX DRAKOS SERIES (11 BOOKS)
THE OZ DRAKOS SERIES (2 BOOKS)
THE MONK PALETTI SERIES (2 BOOKS)
THE PRESIDENT'S GIRLFRIEND SERIES (8 BOOKS)
THE PRESIDENT'S BOYFRIEND SERIES (1 BOOK)
THE RAGS TO ROMANCE SERIES (23 BOOKS)

HOLIDAY SPECIALS:
***GIRLS ON THE RUN*:**
A GABRINI VALENTINE
AND
***GUNS AND ROSES*:**
A SINATRA AND GABRINI CHRISTMAS

**STANDALONE BOOKS:
BONITA SINATRA: TO CATCH A
JOCK
ROMANCING MO RYAN
MAEBELLE MARIE**

TABLE OF CONTENTS

PROLOGUE

"Where's Marti? Go get Marti!"

Eric Peterson hurriedly opened the sliding glass door and yelled for his friend, and the party's host, to come outside.

Marti Nash had just walked in to grab more drinks for the coolers when Eric yelled her name. Worried that some of her daughter's friends might be getting too rowdy, she turned back around and hurried outside.

"What is it?" she asked Eric as soon as she stepped out onto the patio. They were in her backyard, celebrating her daughter's sweet sixteen birthday, and young people were everywhere. Some were in the pool. Some were playing chess on one end of the patio while there was a card game going on the other end. It was loud outside and fun-filled, but what she didn't see was anybody being rude or rowdy. "Why did you call me out here? I was getting more drinks."

"Look."

"Look at what?"

"Look!" Eric turned Marti in the direction where she could see across the far end of her backyard. That was when she saw Kamille

Oliver, her best friend, walking across the lawn with Andy Sloan. And Marti couldn't believe it. "Oh no she didn't!"

"Why would she bring him here?" Eric asked. "She knows you can't stand that man."

"Be nice, Ma." Jaleesa Nash, Marti's daughter, hurried over to her. They said she looked just like her mother, but Marti could never see it. "I mean it, Ma. He's just being nice. You be nice too."

"And you stay away from him," Marti admonished her daughter.

But when Andy yelled out, "*Is that my little Jaleesa over there,*" her daughter smiled and hurried to him. She vigorously embraced the man that used to be her mother's patrol partner for nearly five years, and was considered a member of the family, before Marti requested and received a different partner. Everybody knew Marti despised him.

But Andy seemed as oblivious as Jaleesa. He was smiling as he hugged Marti's daughter. "Long time, no see, fly girl," he said as they rocked each other side to side the way they used to do. "It's been too long. Way too long! And look how big you've gotten," he added as he pulled back and looked down the length of her. "You're a big girl now!"

Then he glanced over at Marti. "Hey

Markita." He said it with that grin she hated. "Still looking good I see," he added, looking up and down her body. They never slept together, nor came close to doing so, but she was certain he told people that they had. That was the kind of man he was.

And Marti wasn't playing along. "Can I talk to you?" she said to Kamille, the woman that had brought him there. Without cracking a smile, Marti reopened her sliding glass door and stepped inside without waiting for a response from her best friend.

"And hello to you too," Kamille said sarcastically as she followed Marti into the house.

But as soon as she walked into the kitchen and closed the sliding glass door, Marti let her have it. "Why did you bring that bastard to my house?"

"You mean your partner?"

"My *ex*-partner. And he's *ex* for a reason. He's a jealous, slimy bastard and you know it."

"Who wouldn't be jealous? He's still a beat cop and you're already a detective lieutenant. I'm jealous too!"

"He claims I *earned* what I have by sleeping my way to the top. You know he said that, right?"

"Girl, everybody knows Andy just be running his mouth. He said the same thing about me when I became a detective. He says a lot of things. Why you take him so seriously?"

"I take everybody seriously. I don't put anything past anybody."

"Except for me, of course," Kamille said with her high-wattage smile.

Marti couldn't help but smile too. They'd been best friends since grade school. Went through the police academy together. "Except for you, child," she said, and they laughed.

"By the way," asked Kamille, "have you heard anything?"

"About what?"

"About how I did on the sergeant's exam?"

"Child no, and stop changing the subject. Why did you bring him here? You know I don't roll with crooked cops like that. They wanna keep guys like him on the force? Fine. Keep'em. I don't have any jurisdiction over those hiring and firing decisions. But I'm not letting cops like that hang around me or mine. And you know how I feel about that. Why did you bring him here, Mill?"

"He missed you and Jaleesa. You used to treat him like he was a member of your family. Like he was your brother and Jaleesa's uncle. Then you wouldn't even talk to him anymore."

"That's before I found out who he really was. That's before I saw him taking a bribe right in front of me."

"Internal Affairs investigated and said he's clean."

"That's because they're dirty too," Marti proclaimed.

Kamille laughed, which caused Marti to smile. "You need to get over yourself, and I'm not joking," Kamille added. "Andy's been a good cop for seven long years. He was your partner for five of those years. Then he has one little hiccup and you kick him to the curb? That ain't right. I'm sorry, but that ain't right. He just wanted to drop by and wish Jaleesa a happy sixteenth, that's all he wanted to do. He hasn't seen her in years, thanks to you. What's so wrong with that, Marti?"

"A crooked cop is a crooked cop is a crook. I don't want my child to have anything to do with somebody who takes an oath to defend and protect and all he's doing is lining his pockets. That's what's wrong with it."

The sliding glass door opened, and Eric peeped inside. He looked nastily at Kamille. "You okay, Marti?" He could see Marti was

13

visibly upset.

"Yeah, I'm . . ." Marti couldn't lie and say she was good because she wasn't. "What's up?"

"Sorry to disturb you, but we're out of drinks."

"I'll bring some out."

Eric looked at Kamille nastily again. "Sure you're okay?"

"Boy bye!" said Kamille, offended.

"You don't talk to me that way," Eric shot back.

"You don't talk to me that way either. Yeah I brought Andy over here. What's the big damn deal?"

"You know Marti doesn't want him here. You know that!"

"I'll bring the sodas out, Eric," Marti said to end the back and forth. Eric gave Kamille another hard look and then retreated back outside, sliding the door shut behind him.

"Who does he think he's talking to?" Kamille asked. "I'm a Detective in the Memphis Police Department, thank you very much. He's got some nerve. He don't know me like that."

Marti began walking toward the frig. "Just get Andy away from my house," she said as she began pulling out a 24-pack of canned sodas in a long carton. "I don't want that kind of dirty around my child."

"Your child," asked Kamille, "or your career?"

Marti looked at her best friend. They were both ambitious as hell and never tried to hide it. They both wanted to be at the top of their profession. But Marti's moral core always remained intact. On that she did not compromise. "I don't want him around my child *and* my career," she said. Then she looked at Kamille. "Why would you and your career want to be around a piece of filth like him anyway?"

"Why do you think? He's cute. For a bougie brother, he ain't bad looking at all." Kamille nor Marti liked *bougie brothers*. They were too soft, too self-centered, too dainty for their taste. "I'm not like you, Marti. I can't live without a man for years on end. I'm sorry. But I can't do it. I have gots to have that hood."

Marti frowned. "Hood? Andy's bougie. He's no hood rat."

"I didn't say nothing about no hood rats."

"Then what hood are you talking about?"

"That *manhood*," Kamille said, pointing to her midsection. "That's the only hood I'm interested in. *Man*hood. And yes, I gots to have that. And the bigger the better. The meatier the better."

"Okay, okay, I get it," Marti said with a smile.

"And it don't get any bigger and meatier than Andy's, I'm here to tell you right now."

"So that's all it takes for you? He's good in bed?"

Kamille looked at her friend. "You are so hard, you know that? Always was and always will be. You expect too much from these men out here. That's why you haven't had a long-term relationship since Rog. Since Jaleesa's father. They're *men*, Markita! Men! You can't expect too much out of no man."

Marti shook her head. "That's crazy."

Kamille was offended by what she saw as a crass, *I'm better than you* response. "I'm not like you, okay? I'm not perfect like you."

But Marti shot back. "I'm not perfect, either, and never tried to be."

"I need a man, okay?" Kamille was blunt. "I gots to have a man. I'll do anything to keep me a man."

"Including diving to the bottom of the barrel and dragging Andrew out?"

"Including that, yes ma'am, yes ma'am. He's good in bed? And cute? Hell to the yes! Let it be known that I, Kamille Oliver, will dive to the bottom of any barrel if he checks both those boxes." Then Kamille smiled. "I do have

16

my standards you know."

Marti shook her head and laughed as she grabbed another case of sodas out of the frig. "You don't be about nothing good. That's what I know!"

"Got that right," Kamille said with a laugh of her own. "Oh, by the way, you were right."

"Take this outside," Marti said as she pushed one of the cases of sodas toward the opposite side of the counter. "What was I right about?"

"About the Evans case," Kamille said as she walked over to the countertop. "He didn't do it."

Marti looked at Kamille. "But everybody on your team were convinced he was guilty as sin."

"*I* was convinced he was guilty as sin too. Wasn't just my team. I was convinced too. But he wasn't guilty. The DNA came back last night. And guess who done it?"

"His roommate."

"Just like you said," said Kamille as she nodded her head. "I don't know how you do it, girl, but you got a knack for solving these complex cases."

"Wasn't nothing complex about the Evans case. Just a group of cops too willing to roll with the obvious rather than with the truth."

"Count me among them," said Kamille, raising her hand. "You're the best cop on the force. Period. You could be chief someday. You got what it takes. That's what you ought to shoot for."

"And give up day-to-day police work to be a paper-pusher?" Marti shook her head. "Not a chance."

"But aren't you afraid you're as high as they're gonna let you go? Because let's face it, girl, the MPD is still a good old boys' network. They might be black boys, but they're still good and old."

Marti laughed.

"And they don't treat neither one of us with the respect we deserve. They look at us like okay, we're smart black women, but we're *women*. And women should never get ahead of them. So who did we sleep with to get the promotions we have gotten? That's how they think. I get that all the time, and I know you get it even more so. Hell, we didn't have to sleep with anybody to get where we are. And I'm getting tired of them claiming we have. But we put up with it like it's nothing."

"I never said it was nothing," Marti admitted.

"And you got everything going for you:

You're gorgeous. Which I am too, by the way," Kamille added with a grin. "But you're next level gorgeous even though you don't believe it."

Marti didn't believe it and never would, even though men declared it all the time. But to her the mirror didn't lie. When she looked in it, she saw a frightened kid staring back at her, not some bombshell like they claimed.

But Kamille kept on singing her praises. "Not that I don't have it going on too, don't get it twisted. But you have that perfect slenderness with your curves. Whereas I left slender behind a decade ago, and it ain't coming back no time soon. I'm getting that middle-age spread."

"Thirty-three is not middle age, Kamille. We're thirty-three. We're not old."

"You know what I mean! But you're the total package. And you're smarter than any of those guys on the force will ever be. And you're athletic too."

Marti smiled. "*What*? I am not athletic!"

"But you look in shape, that's all I'm saying. You're the best we have to offer and those guys don't appreciate it. I don't get that."

Marti grabbed the second case of sodas and began to head for the exit. "Nothing to get," she said, although it was a painful truth she had to deal with on a daily. "We love our jobs. Why be upset because some man won't put respect on our names? Bump that!"

"The two favorite words of losers," she said as she grabbed a case of sodas and followed Marti.

"But getting back to the point." Marti stopped walking and looked sincerely at her best friend. "Get Andy away from my house. For real. Find an excuse, do whatever you have to do, but get him gone. He's bad news."

"What's so bad news about him? That's what I don't understand. He's never done anything to you or Jaleesa. You're just going by your gut again. Without any proof of any corruption whatsoever."

Marti looked at her with that serious look on her face she was known for. "I saw him collect a big money bribe from a hapless storeowner who didn't have money to be giving to no crooked cop. I saw it with my own two eyes, Kamille! Then he had the nerve to ask if I wanted some too. Like *who does that*? Get him away from my house and my child and I'm not playing. Right is still right and wrong is still wrong."

Kamille frowned. "Damn! What's that?"

Marti was confused. "Right and wrong?" But then she also heard what sounded like a very loud argument going on outside. And one of the voices, the loudest voice she realized, was Andy's. "Oh hell no!" She angrily hurried out of the sliding glass door, with Kamille right behind her. "Coming to my house starting trouble? Oh hell no!"

"You don't know if he started it, Marti." Kamille was hurrying to keep up with her. "Marti, slow your butt down. It's just an argument!"

But as soon as both ladies stepped out onto the patio, Andy stood up from the poker table, pulled out his weapon, and shot the young man he was arguing with. Then he quickly turned his gun toward the other young people at that table, forcing them to flee for their lives.

"Drop that weapon, Andy, what are you doing?" Kamille was crying out as she and Marti dropped their sodas and began pulling out their weapons too. Andy turned his gun toward them as soon as he heard Kamille yelling his name, as if he was ready to fire on her too. But before he could get another shot off, Marti's training kicked in and she knew she had to shoot and shoot to kill. Or be killed. She fired seven consecutive rounds into Andy's body in such rapid succession that it felt to Marti like she only fired once. She took out her former partner, a man she used to respect, easily. He dropped like a sack of potatoes.

But as soon as he did, screams were heard behind him. Bloodcurdling screams. Somebody was down behind him. One or more of her bullets had apparently traveled straight through Andy, and hit an innocent bystander.

Marti's heart dropped. She was neutralizing a threat. She was doing her job. She never meant to hurt any of her daughter's guests!

She and Kamille began running toward the downed young person to render aid: another part of their job. But as soon as Marti realized who that downed young person was, she stopped in her tracks.

She could see people gathering around her child.

She could see Kamille crying and cradling the young girl's head in her lap.

She could hear people yelling to call 911.

She could see young people still screaming from the top of their lungs and holding their hands over their heads and walking around like zombies.

But Marti Nash was unable to move so much as a muscle.

Detective Lieutenant Marti Nash, for the first time in her entire life, was paralyzed with fear.

CHAPTER ONE

FOUR YEARS LATER

He didn't toss. He didn't turn. But man did he dream.

But it wasn't like a dream. It seemed so real, and so vivid, and so horrifyingly horrific that Grant McGraw, the chief of the Belgrave Police Department, flew open his large, bloodshot blue eyes and sat up in bed with a sudden lift up: resting on his elbows. His heart pounding, his breathing strangled and heavy, he realized at once it was another nightmare. Of another drowning. Another fire. Another shooting. Another car wreck. Another, another, another. Night after night after night. When would it ever end?

He laid back down onto his saturated pillow as sweat pierced his pores like a second skin. He lifted his cellphone from his nightstand to check the time. Just after three a.m. He had fallen asleep an hour ago, or maybe not even that long ago. He couldn't remember. Now he was wide awake again. Sleepless in Belgrave again. *When would it ever end*?

He threw the covers off of his naked body and got out of bed. After peeing, he put on his bathrobe, made his way downstairs past his huge living room, around his formal dining room, and into his gourmet kitchen of earth tones browns and grays. Grabbing a bottled beer out of the frig and opening it, he made his way outside onto his large wraparound southern front porch of his large, colonial brick home, leaving his door wide open to let fresh air blow through.

But the silence was startling to his ears. He could hear the wildlife alright. Who couldn't hear the cicadas screaming their love across Florida? Or the crickets and the birds and the frogs and the bees? But he could also hear a leaf drop if it fell from one of the many maple trees in his front yard. Or a feather dropping from a bird. Because all the noise out there was devoid of human noise. Which made it lonely. And tiresome. And as if there was no noise at all.

He took a long gulp of his beer. Then he placed the cold bottle against his forehead. It was still springtime in Florida, but it was hot as hell even that time of morning. Not to mention that nightmare that drenched him, too, as if it had actually happened, even though it was just a dream.

Across the street were thick woods that used to feel comforting to Grant. Like his own isolated piece of the world where no one could bother him or people-watch him or blame him. But now as he sat in the dark in that early morning hour, those same woods felt ominous. Like they were closing in on him too. Like they wanted their pound of flesh from him too.

He looked up at the massive Tuscan columns on his front porch that redefined the architectural design of his home, and it suddenly seemed as if they could fall down and crush him at any moment. As if they could close in on him too. He was forty-eight years old, staring in the dark because he couldn't find an hour's peace in bed, and it felt as if this was as good as it was going to get for him. Sitting on his own front porch afraid of the woods and quietness. This was all? *This was it*?

He drank all of his beer: he was drinking way too much and knew it. Wasn't doing himself any favors and he knew that too. But he was getting to a place, or might already be there, where he just didn't give a damn.

He went back inside, tossed his bottle in the trash filled with other empty bottles just like it, and showered and got ready for work.

At least he had work.

CHAPTER TWO

Why would a former police lieutenant take a job that barely pays above minimum wage?

And at her age too?

Was she fired?

Did she quit before she got fired?

Did she sleep her way to the top and got caught?

What's her story? Everybody's got one.

She heard the whispers on a daily basis

and saw the fingers pointing and elbows knocking every time she walked past one of her much younger colleagues. It was a new position in the state of Florida, that of a police consultant, and almost all of those hired were kids straight out of college looking to pad their resumes as they waited for far better positions in a recession where jobs were scarce. There were others, however, who were there because they were old and just plain broke and anything would do. That was Marti.

At thirty-seven, she was old compared to most of her young colleagues, and she was definitely broke after years of living off her savings and barely able to get out of bed to get a real job. Three-and-a-half years ago she decided she couldn't do it anymore. She sold her home at a loss because of what happened there, and left Memphis and Tennessee for good. She drifted from state to state and town to town, looking for a place to call home, but she'd always end up feeling out of place. Then she'd move to yet another town in yet another state and the disconnected feelings continued.

But once her savings were completely exhausted, she had no option but to get it together and get back to work. Being a cop was out of the question. Although that was all she knew, she knew she could never go back to that. But being a police consultant? Unlike her young colleagues who didn't know squat about real police work, she could consult with both hands behind her back. She knew what she was doing. That was why she believed, as her very first assignment, they gave her the worst case of police incompetence any of them had ever heard of.

But as she drove past the *Welcome to Belgrave* sign, it was also clear that knowing what she was doing and loving what she was doing were two different things. Some days she understood why she was living paycheck to paycheck and was okay with it. She understood how she got where she was. She understood she was just getting back on her feet. But other days she still couldn't believe this was what her life had devolved into. Four years ago she was a lieutenant in Tennessee and well on her way to yet another promotion. Now she was a low-paying consultant in Florida driving into a town she'd never heard of before she got the assignment.

And even after she looked it up, she was surprised to learn that it had nearly fifty thousand residents and wasn't some super-tiny little nothing town as she had assumed. But it also had a lot of crime, among the worse stats in the state, and a longstanding mid-sized

29

police force so badly run that it astounded her still.

That was why she drove right past the Belgrave Police Department to conduct a tour of the city for herself. But not before noticing that the space marked for *Chief of Police* had what looked like a brand-new Mercedes-Maybach parked there. Which just screamed corruption to her. How in the world could the chief of a town this size afford a car like that? But she kept on driving.

Jake Crocker, the Assistant Attorney General that oversaw the consultant program, said Belgrave was a nice, clean town that she would love. And when she first arrived, it appeared to be exactly that. Nice. Clean. And very white. Not all, but nearly all. On *that* side of town.

On *that* side of town she saw a thriving city with gorgeous buildings like the convention center and the museum, and beautiful homes with landscaped lawns and tree-lined streets, and nice, three-to-four-star hotels galore. Plenty of space. Plenty of room to roam.

But she kept driving because she knew better. She came from the other side of town. That was why she looked for the tracks. And once she found them and drove over those railroad tracks, she saw that other side of town.

On that *other* side of town was adject poverty of a staggering degree. The mangy dogs running loose and wild. The filth and the trash. The stray cats everywhere. The children playing soccer on dirt roads and grown men sitting under shade trees playing checkers while their women sat on dilapidated porches and decks playing cards. From the mostly white trailer park poverty to the mostly black clapboard house poverty, they were all stacked there together with too little room to roam and not enough room to even *feel* free.

It was a study in complete contrast compared to the gorgeously appointed streets that visitors first viewed when they entered the town. But Marti knew there had to be another side because she'd seen it too many times before. Like going to Asia where all you saw were immaculately clean streets and the marvel of architectural design and light and glam galore. Until you kept driving. Then you saw the *real* town.

Marti was seeing the real town where she'd say at least two-thirds of the Belgrave population lived. It was a tale of two cities in one town. And she'd bet the bank that it was that other side of town that comprised that forty-nine percent wrongful incarceration rate she was there to investigate. No question about it. She'd bet the farm on it too.

She hooked a U-turn, decided it was time to check in, and made her way back toward the Belgrave Police Department to announce her arrival. And it was going to be a very unceremonious welcome she was sure.

CHAPTER THREE

Although Grant McGraw was the chief of the Belgrave Police Department, he had not heard about any consultant coming to his jurisdiction at all. He was in his regular morning meeting with his senior leadership staff: his captain and lieutenants and their recorder: Sergeant Carter. They met in the Chief's office every morning to review the overnight stats. It had been another bad night in Belgrave. Including ninety-eight burglaries.

"Ninety-eight?" Grant was astounded.

"And those are the ones we know about," said Carter. "More reports may be coming in later. It's a major problem nowadays. Might be a ring, an outside gang, but we don't know that yet. There were also forty-seven assaults."

"Anybody dead is the question?" asked Captain Ryan Jeffers, called Cap by the front-line employees, or RJ by those who knew him well. The only African American, and Grant's second-in-command, on the force.

"There were no deaths. But get this," said Carter. "We had sixty-six DV calls overnight."

Nobody could believe it. "Damn," said RJ. "Domestic Violence is the thing now? That number keeps rising every single week."

"Have you seen some of these wives lately?" asked Lieutenant Pete Kerrigan, affectionately called *Lieutenant Pete* by his men. Pushing sixty, he was the oldest person in the room and one of the oldest on the force. "It's no wonder husbands are beating the crap out of them."

The men laughed. Grant, who didn't crack a smile, tossed another NoDoz into his cup of coffee.

RJ picked up on it as soon as he did it. "Another sleepless night, Chief?"

"Does he ever sleep?" asked Pete. "I heard he was here before four a.m. this morning."

Before Grant could address their comments, which he had no intentions of addressing anyway, his office door flung open and Mayor Dooney Rickter walked in. The men that sat in front of Grant's desk all quickly stood to their feet.

RJ slapped on that fake smile the townspeople loved. "Good morning, Mayor!"

"How you doing, RJ? Saw you on the links yesterday. You need help."

RJ laughed. "I hear I'm doing better

than you."

"You are. But that don't mean you don't need help."

RJ laughed again. It was expected of him.

"Good morning, Mayor," various others in the room said, too, attempting to get on the mayor's good side, but he ignored the rest of them. Everybody knew RJ was his favorite. The mayor had wanted to appoint RJ as chief years ago, but the old guard in town, the members of the Belgrave Oversight Board (the *BOBs,* as they were called), wouldn't hear of it. They wanted Grant McGraw. He, they felt, was one of them. Dooney tossed a red folder on his desk.

Grant, who sat behind the desk, didn't touch it. "What's this?"

"We got trouble." They all looked at the mayor. "That's what it is."

"If you're talking about the overnight stats," Grant started, but Dooney cut him off.

"You think I'd waste my time coming here about some overnight stats?"

Grant, now concerned, looked at the folder, but still didn't touch it. "What kind of trouble are you talking about then?"

"It's been nearly two years since that deranged governor of ours ordered every police department in the state to submit DNA samples in every single case where there was evidence capable of being tested. You remember that?"

Grant nodded. "I remember."

"Well the results are in. Boy are they in. Tallahassee's going ballistic. Effective immediately, every police department in the state of Florida that placed poorly will get a so-called police consultant shoved down our throats to reverse the troubling trends."

"Make yourself plain, Dooney." Grant hated the mayor's histrionics. "What are you talking about?"

"Those DNA test results proved that many men and ladies currently incarcerated in this state didn't do the crime. The DNA, at least as far as our progressive governor is concerned, exonerates them."

"How many people are we really talking about, Mayor?" RJ asked him. "Can't be *that* many."

"That's where you're wrong, RJ." The mayor looked flustered. "It's way more than you think. But that's not even the worst of it."

"What is it?" asked Grant.

"They ranked each police department based on their percentage of exonerations. A high exoneration percentage puts you near the bottom. A low exoneration percentage puts you near the top, which is where every department wants to be."

"Let me guess," said Lieutenant Pete. "We were near the bottom?"

"Near it? No. We *ARE* the bottom!"

Everybody stiffened. "We are?" asked RJ.

"What was our percentage?" Grant asked.

"Forty-nine percent," said the mayor. "Forty-doggone-nine percent!"

They were all floored. The men looked at each other, and then at their boss. But Grant was looking at *his* boss, the mayor. "Are you telling me that forty-nine percent of the perpetrators my department arrested were exonerated after their DNA was tested?"

"That's what I'm telling you. That's exactly what I'm telling you." They could tell the mayor was livid. "You don't just have a bad rate. You have the worst rate in the entire state!" The mayor yelled this out. "Numeral uno is this police department. You're the worst of the worst. And not by a little bit either. The next worse has an eighteen percent exoneration rate. Just eighteen percent. When we're at FORTY-NINE PERCENT!" He yelled it out again. "Nearly half of everybody you arrested and are now incarcerated are innocent and, after a judge reviews their cases, will undoubtedly be freed! This is a public relations nightmare!"

Grant was devastated, but he didn't let his men see it. His men weren't devastated, because it didn't happen on their watch, but they were equally shocked. And RJ, as usual, summed it up. "We knew we weren't the best police force," he said, "but *damn*!"

"That's why I took the time out of my busy schedule to come down here," Dooney said. "This is not a trial run. This is the real deal. Governor Chauncey Devere has made clear that if this department doesn't clean up its act, the state will take over the running of our entire force. And he'll be glad to do it too. His ass knows I'm running for governor next year. But he can't run against me, so he wants Jake Crocker, his assistant AG, to run against me. He knows I'm more popular than old Jake will ever be, so they need to tarnish me as much as they can. Make no mistake about it. He'll be glad to take over anything I'm in charge of just to show I don't know what the hell I'm doing."

The mayor looked at the chief. "Over my dead body he'll take over this department. You hear me, McGraw? Over my dead body he will."

Then the mayor exhaled to calm himself back down. "In the back of that folder, after the results, is the consultant the AG's office hired to assist us. Which means she can't be that good if they gave her to us."

"She's hired to do what exactly?" asked Grant.

"To consult. To find out what's wrong with y'all and why y'all keep arresting innocent people! What do you think she's here to do? To nursemaid you?"

"Just because those tests says that the DNA wasn't theirs," said Pete, "that don't mean they're all innocent."

Grant rolled his eyes. The mayor gave Pete a chilling look. "And I wonder why my police department is dead last. Only a fool like you would say a fool thing like that, Lieutenant. We're dead last because we have idiots like you in high positions!"

Then the mayor calmed back down again and looked at Grant. "Listen to the consultant."

"Arriving when?"

"Bright and early tomorrow morning."

"Tomorrow?" Grant had not expected to hear that. "That soon?"

"I told you Governor Devere will do

anything in his power to destroy me. Did you hear anything I just said? Yes tomorrow! So clean up your act." Then the mayor just stared at Grant. "Look at you. Unshaven. Bloodshot eyes. Wrinkled suit. When we were in high school you were the quarterback. You were the one voted best dressed and most likely to succeed and all that other bull-crap. Now look at you. Look like you just rolled out of bed and came to work. This department is a disgrace and you know why? Because you, their leader, is a disgrace. Which means I'm a disgrace for being forced to hire your sorry ass. Clean this shit up, McGraw. And I mean now!"

Then the mayor left the office, slamming the door behind him.

CHAPTER FOUR

A silence fell over the room after the mayor slammed the door shut. But when RJ asked to see who this *consultant* was and Grant opened the folder to the last page to see just who it was, too, they all gathered around his desk. The picture staring back at them was of a black woman seemingly in her mid-to-late thirties. She had a proud disposition about her. Sophisticated. Overly-serious, it seemed to Grant, as if she was trying too hard to not try too hard.

But his men saw something altogether different. "I knew it!" said Pete as soon as he saw that face. "A diversity hire. That's what they give us: a diversity hire. All we need!"

Nobody bothered to even look at RJ when Pete made that disparaging comment because RJ, despite sharing the same ethnic background as the consultant, acted more like one of them.

"I heard those gals could be some bossy-ass women if you let'em," said another lieutenant.

"Black women?" Carter spoke as if he was the expert. "They're something else. Mad

41

all the time and bossy as hell. You're right about that." Then he smiled. "Is that why you married a white woman, RJ?"

RJ smiled, too, but it didn't reach his eyes. But they didn't know that. All they knew was that they could kid him like that. All they knew was that he was one of them.

No. She didn't have an overly serious look, Grant decided on second thought as he continued to stare at the consultant's photograph. She had a haunted look. An overly traumatized look. As if she was trying too hard to not be exposed.

"She's probably the worse consultant in America," said Pete, "and they throw her at us. And a woman of all people."

"And not just a woman," said Carter. "A so-called *woman of color*, like we whites ain't got no color. A doggone ni--"

Carter managed to stop himself from going that low, and some in the room did glance at RJ. But RJ seemed oblivious to any of it.

But Grant wasn't. "Okay that's enough," he said before it got down in the sewer any further than it already had.

"But can you believe this, Chief?" Carter said to him, tone deaf. "They gonna slap a ni--"

"I said that's enough, Sergeant Carter!" Grant looked squarely at his sergeant. "Get back to work. All of you!"

"But what you gonna do about it, Chief?" asked another cop.

The chief looked at him. He quickly cowered and began leaving with the rest of his colleagues. When they had gone, Grant looked at RJ, who remained behind. "Why do you let those assholes get away with that racist dribble?"

"The same reason you let'em get away with it," RJ responded. "I'm ambitious. I'm not letting these nobody racist rednecks stop my climb. They can say whatever they want. I'm moving on up."

The two men looked at each other. They understood each other. Then they both looked back at that picture staring at them.

"Think she'll help?"

"No," Grant said bluntly. "But it is what it is."

"Can you imagine? For us to be at the bottom like that? Forty-nine percent of our arrests were dead wrong and very likely will be overturned on appeal because of this new evidence."

Grant leaned back. He was still digesting it too.

"If what Dooney says is true," said RJ, "that means we're routinely arresting the wrong people. We're putting innocent men and women in jail like it's normal."

"It's normal to the men in this department. Think about it, RJ. We've been arresting innocent people at a rate unheard of anywhere in the world probably, and what did they get out of all that horrible news? The fact that the consultant is a black woman! That's their takeaway. Not the horrible stats. But race and gender. That's what we're dealing with here."

Then his anger came from out of nowhere like aways and he grabbed a stack of files on his desk and threw them against the wall, with papers flying everywhere.

As soon as it happened, the office door opened quickly, and Sergeant Carter peeped inside. "We got a mass casualty event at the Wafer House on Ridge Cove, sir."

Grant and RJ were astonished. "Mass casualty?" asked Grant.

"Are you sure?" asked RJ.

"I'm positive," said Carter.

Grant, still stunned, jumped to his feet. "Get every available unit to the scene," he ordered Carter as he grabbed his suit coat from the back of his chair. They'd never had a mass casualty anything in Belgrave before. It was foreign to them. Grant and RJ began hurrying out of the office.

"Should I call those out on vacation back in, sir?" Carter asked, running behind them.

"Not until I assess the situation," Grant said, putting on his suitcoat. "Just get all available units over there now."

"Yes sir," Carter said, and hurried to do as he was ordered.

"I'm riding with you. Let me grab my phone," RJ said as he hurried to his desk.

Grant kept walking, hurrying out of the same doors Marti Nash was about to walk into. She and Grant nearly collided. But Marti saw the big man coming before he saw her and she was able to move out of his way just in time, prompting Grant to put the brakes on his fast walking too.

But when he stopped, he stopped right next to her. They were within an inch of each other.

And as soon as Grant saw her, it felt as if a kind of warmth entered his body. Like a feeling of something familiar. The feeling of finding something near and dear to his heart, and feeling responsible for what he'd found. It was so out of nowhere odd and strange but so lovely, too, that it threw him for a loop.

But Marti was too focused on her assignment to be thrown. All she saw was an unshaven white man in his late forties or maybe even fifty with unusually deep-blue but bloodshot eyes standing before her. She got the sense that most ladies might find him most attractive, in a shabby-chic way, but to her he wasn't at all that well put together. She saw a scattered man. A disorganized man. A man in a rush, but too slow to get there. And she recognized his face from the background materials she'd been given. His eyes gave him away. "Chief McGraw?"

Grant stared at her. Had he met her before? And then he suddenly recognized her too! And it was that recognition that snapped him out of his *staring unblinkingly at her* stupor and propelled him forward. Getting all warm and bubbly over some doggone consultant? The very woman that could write a report that could take his department away from him? Had he lost all his marbles??? "You're supposed to be here tomorrow," he said.

"That's correct, sir, but I wanted to get an early start."

As RJ hurried out of the station, Grant began hurrying down the steps toward his car, his suit coat flapping as he walked.

Marti glanced at RJ, a tall, slender, very

46

attractive black man. She didn't know who he was although he was staring hard at her the way blue eyes had done. But she had to present her credentials to the head man. And according to her papers, it was the man she recognized as the chief. She hurried behind him. "I'm Markita Nash, sir. I've been assigned by the Attorney General's office as consultant for this jurisdiction."

"I know who you are."

Then why don't you stop for two seconds, she wondered, as she had to hurry to keep up with the big man's long strides. "Have you been called out on a case, sir?"

Grant didn't answer.

"I may as well join you," Marti suggested as Grant and RJ hopped into the Mercedes-Maybach that was parked in the space reserved for the Chief of Police. It was the same car she had noted earlier as far too expensive for a police chief to afford. And although he had to have heard her suggestion that she ride along with him, Grant, behind the wheel, sped away. He left her standing in the very dust his car was kicking up.

Marti was pissed. Though not surprised. It was exactly what she expected from this broken-down department. And that chief? Rot always started at the top. But she was hired to do a job and she was going to do it. She ran to her aging Dodge Charger that was parked a few feet over, hopped in, and took off after the chief.

CHAPTER FIVE

RJ, seated on the passenger seat, saw her through the rearview mirror. "She's following us."

Grant had already noticed. But he got on the radio with Sergeant Carter. "Any units on the scene yet?"

"Three are already there. They have the gunman in handcuffs isolated in a room. They're waiting on you."

"Okay good. And tell them no Miranda until I get there. Don't ask him any damn questions. Don't blow it."

"Yes, sir."

"What have they assessed?"

"Loads of shots fired. Many wounded."

"Any deaths?"

"Yes sir. At least two people. Maybe more."

"*Damn*," said RJ.

"Call other jurisdictions. Tell them to get ambulances to the scene too."

"Will do, Chief," said Carter, and Grant ended the communication.

"Damn," said RJ again. Then he looked

through his rearview again. "Not a bad looking chick."

Grant frowned. "What?"

"That consultant," said RJ, still looking out of his rearview. "She's a nice-looking girl. I mean, she looked nice on her photo. But not like that! That photo doesn't do her any justice."

Grant shook his head. Two people dead, many wounded, and his second-in-command can only talk about a woman. And a consultant at that!

"I'm going to tap that for sure," RJ was saying.

Grant rolled his eyes and sped up.

But RJ kept talking. "I'm going to see what that tastes like for sure," he added with a smile. "I haven't had me any pure brown sugar in a long, long time. I'm gonna hit that real hard."

Then Grant blurted out, "*You stay away from her,*" before he realized he'd said it.

RJ looked at Grant and grinned. "Alright, I see you. Chief. You want first dibs. Okay. You earned the right. You got first. But let's be clear: I got next. You hear me? I got next!"

Grant's jaw tightened. He knew RJ and every other married man on the force had side pieces all over the place. But for him to think that a serious lady like that consultant was going to be that easy to conquer angered him. What did he think she was? One of those ladies of the evening they all frequented at Ma Bev's every now and again? She was not that! And RJ even thinking that she was angered Grant. For some reason it angered him mightily.

But when Grant could hear and then see police cars all over the Wafer House restaurant on Ridge Cove, he forgot about RJ and that consultant and everything else they were talking about and raced to the scene. He and RJ hopped out and hurried toward the entrance.

When Marti arrived shortly after them she parked and hopped out of her car, too, as a cop opened the yellow tape and allowed Grant and RJ passage through. But he closed the tape right back as Marti hurried up behind them. "I'm with Chief McGraw," she said to the officer.

"And I'm BiBi Netanyahu," said the officer.

Marti, finding him ridiculous, yelled out beyond him. "*Chief*!"

Although Grant didn't stop walking

toward the entrance, he turned around. Had his officer stopped any other so-called consultant from entering the crime scene, he would have given him a heartfelt attaboy. But when he saw Marti's so-serious face staring at him with that plea in her massive eyes, as if she wanted him to understand that she didn't sign up to be disrespected by his men, he understood it. He didn't understand why he understood it. She was the enemy as far as he was concerned. But he understood it. "She's with me," he yelled to his officer.

When the now-stunned officer heard the chief's reply, he quickly lifted the tape so that Marti could go under. Relieved, she hurried behind the chief, determined to stay close to him.

But as they surveyed the crime scene that still had blankets over the deceased, and as paramedics were still assessing the wounded, a detective came out of a side room where a short, white man in jeans and a black blazer was seated. From the open door, Marti could see that he was smoking a cigarette and drinking a coke.

"That our perp?" Grant asked his detective as he looked at the man too.

"That's him."

"Have you asked him anything?"

"Nothing, sir."

"Has he said anything?"

"Just that he's innocent. That he didn't do it. Which is laughable since at least five witnesses said he was the shooter."

"Are you sure they got it right?"

Grant and RJ were stunned to hear the consultant's voice. They looked at Marti. The detective did too. "What do you mean are they sure?" RJ asked her.

"Who is she anyway?" the detective asked.

"She's that consultant," said RJ. "A know-it-all consultant."

"Look lady," the detective said nastily, "why don't you go in the corner like a good little girl and consult, and let us grownups do the hard police work alright?"

"Just because Chief let you through that tape doesn't mean you get a say in our investigations," RJ added.

The detective was even more upset. "Our hands are full trying to deal with this disaster and you have the nerve to ask me if we're sure a man five people said pulled the trigger might be telling the truth and all the witnesses are liars?"

"I didn't call anybody a liar," Marti pointed out. "I was just saying--"

"You don't need to say anything but get out of the way," the detective said. "This is my crime scene. Now scat!"

"Put a lid on it, Dawson," the chief ordered his detective.

RJ and the detective glanced at each other, and then at Grant. "This okay with you, Chief?" asked RJ.

It wasn't okay with him at all. He didn't like the fact that Marti was intruding in their crime scene either. But she didn't come across to him as a frivolous person. They're the ones arresting innocent people, not her. They're the ones with the horrible record. She saw something that they, namely he, might have missed. "Why do you think the witnesses could be wrong?"

"Look at all those bullet holes," Marti said.

All three men, two of which didn't want to give her even that legitimacy, looked.

"You see the trajectory," said Marti. "If you're righthanded, those holes by virtue of how they were shot will have a right slant. If you're lefthanded, those holes will have a left slant."

The detective couldn't believe such craziness. "That's utter nonsense!"

"*Bullet slants*? Really?" RJ couldn't

believe it either. "Is this what we're doing?"

But Grant wasn't ready to dismiss her out of hand. He hadn't noticed before, but he now could see what she was saying. "Let's say you're right," he said. "How would that make our suspect innocent?"

"And all five of our witnesses wrong?" added RJ.

"That man over there, in that room, is righthanded," Marti said.

"How would you know?" asked the angry detective.

"He's smoking with his right hand. He's holding his soda with his right hand."

"This is nuts!" said the detective in charge. "He could be both left-and-right handed for all you know!"

"An ambidextrous shooter cannot consistently have a lefthanded slant. The slant will be more ambiguous. At least from what I've seen." She was looking at those bullet holes again. "They wouldn't look like this."

Grant exhaled as he opened his suitcoat and placed his hands on his hips. "Where's the video? Does this place have video?"

"Yes sir," the detective said.

"Have you seen it?"

"Haven't had a chance to, sir. I got here and secured the suspect and the crime scene."

"Where is it?"

"In the manager's office down that hall."

The chief was heading down the hall. RJ and the detective followed him, with RJ ordering two cops to stay with the suspect at all times. "No conversation," he ordered.

But when Marti tried to follow the chief, the detective in charge wouldn't hear of it. "Your ass staying right where you are," he said. Then he ordered another cop to keep her in her place.

But when the chief and his men got in the manager's office and the manager racked up the video to the time of the shooting, they got an eyeful. The perp was a customer. He had apparently eaten his meal and was at the cash register to pay. He was short, white, and wore jeans and a dark blazer.

But after exchanging words with the cashier, he pulled out a gun and fired on her. And aimed his gun on all the other fleeing and screaming customers and started firing on all of them.

But two things were for certain as the chief, RJ, and the detective in charge looked at that video: The man all five witnesses insisted was the perp, and the man the detective was certain was their guy, wasn't. And he most definitely, just as Marti had said, was lefthanded!

The chief looked at his men with disgust on his face. They were about to do it again. They would have hurried out to the media, told them they had the culprit already in custody, and then they would have watched that video in horror. And even worse, had it not been working that day, or had that recording never come to life, an innocent man sitting in that room just might have gone to prison behind their shoddy work!

But that begged the question: If he didn't do it, who did? "Keep it rolling," the chief ordered the store manager.

He kept rolling it. And the chief and his men kept looking to see just where the real gunman had gone. They saw him do his deed, and then they saw him flee out of a side door.

"*Got*dammit!" said Grant. "We've got a gunman on the loose!"

They all hurried up front as Grant got on the radio with Sergeant Carter, ordering a canvassing of the entire area and who they were looking for, while RJ and the detective explained the situation to the cops already on scene and ordered them to hit the streets too. They also ordered a group to go find more video.

Marti at first was confused by the

sudden pickup in activity, until the chief got off of the radio and looked over at her. He didn't say she was right. He didn't have to. The look in his eyes, that they had got it wrong again, said enough. The fact that the chief himself told the man in that side room that he was free to go, said it all.

And for the rest of that day she was left to observe while the chief and all his minions went about their business the way cops normally would at such an enormous crime scene. But this time, she noticed, they weren't trying to wrap it up as if police work was a piece of cake. They were taking their time. They were painstakingly going through the evidence. They were behaving as a department under the microscope should.

For the rest of the day, Grant didn't say another word to Marti. But every time she so much as glanced in his direction, she would catch him staring at her. There would be two detectives explaining what they'd discovered so far, and he'd be listening to them while staring at Marti. Or this group of cops or that group of cops would be talking to the chief about the surveillance cameras or the witnesses or whatever else they needed to talk to their chief about, and he'd be standing in the midst of them, listening to them, but staring at

Marti. Or when he was seated in a chair against the wall, his legs and arms folded: obviously exhausted. But Marti noticed that he was still watching her.

But as Grant sat in a chair against that wall, he wasn't watching her with animosity in his heart as she might have thought. He was watching her because he couldn't take his eyes off of her. And it wasn't because of any of that superficial crap: He could tell already that she didn't view herself as some maven of beauty – although she was. She was strikingly beautiful to Grant. From her smooth, dark-brown skin, to her high cheekbones and perfect lips, to her sultry deep brown eyes, she was stunning to him. But that wasn't the draw. That wasn't what was pulling him to her. There were plenty of stunning-looking ladies in Belgrave, and he could bed most of them with the snap of a finger. And already had.

But he couldn't stop watching Marti because of what he felt inside every time he looked her way. Something came alive in his heart. Something about her intrigued him. Something about her interested him for the first time in he couldn't count how many years. Women were to him a transaction. He wined and dined them, or threw money their way when they needed it, and they slept with him.

That was the deal. As simple and as base as that. Which rendered every single relationship he had as artificial. Superficial. Emotionless. *Baseless*.

But this girl? What was going on with *this*? He couldn't figure it out. That was why he stared. That was why every cop in that room kept elbowing each other as they all saw, at one time or another, their chief seemingly mesmerized by the woman they all perceived as nothing more than their archenemy.

Marti felt their hatred too. She felt it to the roots of her hair. Every time a cop looked her way, she saw their sneers. She felt their animosity. They all assumed she was going to write a bad report on their willingness to believe traumatized eyewitnesses so easily, without verifying anything, when they had to know that kind of evidence was among the weakest. And the chief, she assumed, felt the same way his men felt.

But she was also getting a different vibe from the chief. As she continued to walk around and observe, taking mental notes at every turn, she was pleased with at least one thing he did that nobody else in his circle had wanted to do: He listened to her suggestion that they just might have the wrong perp. He listened to her. And then investigated for himself. That said something about his character to her.

But the fact that she knew he had been staring at her so often was because she had been taking a lot of peeps at him herself, said something about her character too. That maybe she wasn't as *over it* with men as she thought she was. That maybe this man, this particular man, had caught her attention when no other man could. But it bothered Marti.

Because it made no sense.

Because she couldn't comprehend for a second why somebody overseeing the worst police department she had ever heard of would catch anything from her but a cold shoulder and a devastating report of incompetence?

That was a different matter altogether.

A matter too deep, too messy, too complicated for her to even try to funnel through.

She kept her distance from that particular man, as she continued to do her job.

CHAPTER SIX

In her hotel room that night, she stood on the balcony, a glass of wine in her hand, and watched the city come to life in lights and traffic. It wasn't a big town, but it was a lively town, and she'd give it high marks for that. But it was nothing like Memphis.

Memphis, she thought. So many things to do. So many places to go. She missed it immensely. But after Jaleesa, it got too big for her. It felt as if she was drowning in it. It felt as if she could no longer function in the city of her birth because everywhere she turned on every street corner, in every marketplace, every club, every school, every grocery store, every theater, all reminded her of her child. Of all those places they used to go. Or where she had to pick her up from. Or where her friends invited her to attend. And she couldn't do it. She just couldn't. She fired the shot that killed her child. How on earth was she supposed to stay there and live there and pretend it didn't happen?

But that was exactly what everyone wanted her to do. To pretend. To push through. To get over it. And when she couldn't, they pretended and pushed through and got over *her*. One day she had mountains of friends. The next day she was all by herself.

She took a sip of her wine and watched the young people stand in line outside a club down the street. They seemed so happy. So full of life. Just like Jaleesa would have been. Because she would have been twenty years old and probably completing her sophomore year of college. Which was supposed to be their grandest time where she would be an adult and they would go from being just mother and daughter, to best friends.

Instead, Jaleesa was gone. Marti was no longer a police officer. And she was standing on the balcony of a town she'd never heard of until she was assigned to its police department, and forced to deal with a man that was as obnoxious as he was thoughtful.

Thoughtful? Was that how she saw him? Just because he listened to a different point of view? Just because he did his job, he was thoughtful? She smiled and shook her head. Had her old friend Kamille been there she would have told her to get a grip. That old white guy was thoughtful? The same guy that left her in the dust when she asked if she could go along with him to the crime scene? *Girl bye*, Kamille would have said. *You need to find yourself a man*!

But even their friendship could not withstand the weight of the guilt Kamille felt for bringing Andy to Jaleesa's sweet sixteen party, and what happened when Andy shot one of the guests, forcing Marti to shoot him.

She leaned her head back and began to move it around as she fought to change the subject. Anything would do.

She continued to look at the young people, and critique their clothing, their body language, even their motivations. Until even that became tiresome. She finished her drink, took another long shower, and then took herself to bed.

She laid in bed, on her side, in the quietness of the night, as a stranger in the night, and cried herself to sleep.

CHAPTER SEVEN

Grant couldn't sleep at all. He tossed and turned. He dreamed another variation of the same dream. The nightmare, he called it. He got up, sat on the side of the bed, and then paced from room to room. He ended up in the kitchen where he always ended up when he just couldn't lay in bed any longer. He grabbed a beer from his frig, and went out onto his front porch.

It was nearly midnight. He could go to the station if he wanted to, but that didn't bring him much comfort either. He could call one of his female friends if he wanted to, and they'd happily agree to meet him at one of the hotels, but he didn't want to be bothered with all that extra either. He didn't want to do or think about anything. It was bedtime for crying out loud! Why couldn't he just take his ass to sleep?

And why, he wondered, was he constantly thinking about that consultant.

About Markita Nash.

She'd been on his mind ever since she steered them away from their usual half-baked, *leaping to conclusions* police work. He studied her the entire time they were at the crime scene. Couldn't take his eyes off of her. Was she a plant the way the mayor seemed to think she was, somebody to stir the pot toward the downfall of the mayor? Grant doubted it. He could tell a mile away that she wasn't the kind of lady that would allow anybody to use her that way.

But that didn't mean she wasn't a problem. She was. One bad report could see his department under the auspices of the state, and him out the door.

He drank his beer and rubbed his eyes. He was tired. He was drained. But he wasn't sleepy.

And that was the problem.

The fact that he couldn't stop thinking about the very woman that could bring his entire department down, and him along with it, was the other problem.

CHAPTER EIGHT

Marti awakened the next day to find that an emergency Zoom meeting had been called of all the assigned police consultants positioned throughout problematic police departments in the state of Florida. The reason? One of their own had been badly beaten by members of a police squad in north Florida. The AG's office sought to reassure the nervous consultants about their right to be at those departments and no bullying or harassment would be tolerated.

Marti, who had more police experience than many of those consultants combined, wasn't nervous at all. After showering and dressing, she sat in her hotel room in front of her computer screen, her coffee in hand, and wished a cop would try to harass her.

But many of her colleagues were not

well-versed in the police culture. They were scared. It was a meeting that took well over seven hours to complete as they covered everything from their planning and replanning, their strategies going forward, to reassurance. Plenty of reassuring. All the other consultants viewed it as a wonderfully clarifying and productive meeting. Marti viewed it as a waste of time.

But after the meeting, she didn't linger. She hurried out of her hotel room, hopped in her car, and made her way to the station. The other consultants had a jumpstart on her already. They had been dispatched to their respective police departments in their respective cities over a week ago. She'd only been on the job in her assigned city one day. And it hadn't exactly been smooth sailing. This was only her second day on the job. She was at a definite disadvantage.

As she drove to the station it was heavily overcast outside, as if the heavens could open up at any second and pour out a mountain of rain. Which was exactly what she didn't need. Because it was the kind of drowsy, sleepy weather she wished she could have taken advantage of and stayed in bed. They didn't want her there. By the way the chief acted yesterday even after she helped their case, meant that he didn't want her there either. And she absolutely didn't want to be there! Sleeping in sounded like a great idea to her. Nobody would care if she showed up or didn't. She even had that long-ass meeting as her excuse. But since nobody on the face of this earth cared about her anyway, she figured she might as well care about herself, and her integrity, and do her job.

She drove even faster.

CHAPTER NINE

It was almost five-thirty when she drove into the parking lot. She was immediately disheartened when she didn't see the Chief's Mercedes parked in his designated space. She would never admit it publicly, but she had been looking forward to seeing his grumpy old ass again. She didn't have an ironclad reason why she wanted to see him again. He wasn't exactly nice to her yesterday. He left her in the dust when she first introduced herself. He never said another word to her even after she tried to help.

But as she watched him throughout that day, she saw something in him that she couldn't verbalize. He wasn't the slouch she expected. He was a leader of men. And he actually listened to her wacky theory about bullet slants that even she would admit wasn't based on scientific fact, but on her own experience as a cop.

She entered the station, walked up to the information desk, and asked if he was in.

"Who's asking?" the clerk on duty asked her.

"Marti Nash."

"That don't tell me much. Unless. . ." Then he grinned the goofiest grin she could imagine. "Are you that diversity hire they been talking about 'round here?"

"Diversity hire? *Really*?" She wasn't even going to mix it up with this buffoon. "Is the chief in?"

The clerk, certain she had to be the one, picked up his desk phone and made a phone call. "Someone will be with you shortly," he said after he ended his call. "Have a seat."

It was their world and she was just visiting, so she took a seat against the wall.

It took several minutes, but Sergeant Carter finally made his way to the front desk. "That her, Sarge?" the clerk asked him.

Carter looked across the lobby and saw her seated there. "That's her all right. May I help you?" he called out to her.

Marti grabbed her thin leather briefcase and made her way back to the desk. "I'm here to see Chief McGraw."

"I'm Sergeant Carter. Are you that consultant?"

"I am, yes." She smiled and extended her hand. "Marti Nash."

Carter wasn't about to shake her hand. How many far more qualified men she had to stomp over to get that job? "You're late."

71

She saw that he wouldn't shake her hand, but she refused to let him shake her smile. She withdrew her hand. "I had an emergency Zoom meeting with the Attorney General's office that was far longer than I had anticipated. I phoned and left a message for the chief. Is he in?"

"Chief already left for the day."

Marti was disappointed. She really wanted to fully introduce herself and get an understanding with the chief about how they planned to work out her involvement, since she was expected to work closely with him. But he was gone already? She'd never known any cop to work a straight nine to five. Especially not one in charge of an entire police department that was already under fire.

Carter, noticing her disappointment, got a bright idea. And he smiled. "He left early, but he'll be happy to meet with you at his house."

The clerk looked at Carter as if he'd just lost his mind. Marti stared at the sergeant. She knew she was being needled. She knew he was lying. "Would he now?" she said to Carter.

"He'll be thrilled! He would love it. Said so himself. Would you like his address?"

He was playing games and she knew it.

But she needed to meet with the chief. And if the chief didn't like the fact that she had come to his home, then she could always blame the sergeant. "I'd love his address," she said, playing right along with them, as the desk clerk held back his laughter, and as Marti took down the address.

CHAPTER TEN

It was nearly six in the evening and pouring sheets of rain by the time Marti made it all the way out to the chief's home. Or was it a mansion?

She couldn't believe how massive his house was. And for the first time she realized this man might have a huge family living there. A wife and a ton of kids. For some crazy reason that never even occurred to her. He looked like a man alone from the first moment she laid eyes on him. Now she realized how shortsighted that was. As if she was projecting onto him something or *somebody* he wasn't. Which she never did. But she did in his case.

But none of that mattered anyway. She needed to meet with the chief and no way was she driving all the way back to town without having an understanding from him about the parameters of her job and how he was technically her boss because she was in his jurisdiction, but he wasn't actually her boss. She was independent. Her only boss was the Assistant Attorney General for the great state of Florida.

But as she sat out in her car and

watched the rain get worse, not better, she decided to make a run for it. She had no umbrella, but she had a briefcase. She placed it over her head as she got out of her car. But as soon as that heavy rain hit her in her face like shards of needles puncturing her with every step she took, she realized it was a mistake. As soon as she realized it was raining, she should have taken her behind back to the hotel and waited to meet with the chief tomorrow.

But she was in it now. Too late to turn back now. She ran all the way from the driveway to the steps, and then all the way up onto his wraparound front porch whose under-hang gave her the first respite from the rain. But she was drenched already from just that little run, and that briefcase had done nothing to shield her hair. She was coming to the man's house looking like Little Orphan Annie ready to burst out and sing: *"The sun'll come out tomorrow. Bet your bottom dollar that tomorrow, they'll be sun!"*

It was all she needed, she thought, as she removed her blouse from tucked inside her slacks and tried to ring the water out of it, and then she tried to fluff-up her fallen hair. But it was no use. She looked like a throwaway. Like Annie. Even her hair had curled up! So she forgot about her appearance and kept her mind singularly focused on why she was there in the first place. She rang his bell.

Inside the house, Grant was in jeans and a sweatshirt preparing his dinner. He loved cooking. It eased his troubled mind. And when it was raining? Heavenly! He loved the rain too. Something about the sound of rain hitting against the windowpanes and to watch it slant through the air reminding man of how powerless and nothing they really were, comforted him. But when he heard his doorbell rang, something he rarely ever heard, he was confounded. Nobody in town had the gall to just drop by his house!

He turned off his pot of stew and made his way around his formal dining room, through his living room, and all the way to his front door. When he saw that consultant through his peephole, he was shocked. What on earth was she doing at his house? Why was she bringing that shit to his home???

Angrily, he flung open his front door.

But as soon as he saw Marti standing there, dripping wet, his heart softened. And as soon as his eyes roamed down to her chest and he saw her nipples full and proud through the wetness of her thin, silk blouse, his midsection went rock hard. Just like that. And those deep feelings that overtook him first at the station the first time he saw her, and again at the Wafer House just from watching her, returned.

Marti saw that flash of anger and annoyance on his face when he first opened that door, and she tried not to focus on anything else. He was pissed by her intrusion at his home and she didn't care that he had softened or gotten excited or any of that. The first impression was always the right one as far as she was concerned. He didn't want her there. He was pissed that she was there. Another place in this world she wasn't welcomed. She couldn't fathom why she thought she just might be welcomed to begin with. But apparently somewhere, in the deep recesses of her heart, she had hoped so.

She put her game face back on. Hardened her exterior. And got on with it. "Hello, Chief. I came because," she started saying, but then she sneezed.

Grant was still trying to digest all that was thrown at him at once: the fact that somebody was standing on his front porch. The fact that *she* was standing on his front porch. The fact that she was turning him on to such an extent that he had to pinch his penis right in front of her to try to settle it back down.

The fact that those other, deeper feelings he couldn't even understand himself had returned. He had too much going on to even hear her say a word to him.

Until she sneezed again.

That angered him. "What are you doing out in this kind of weather anyway?" He grabbed her by the arm and pulled her inside his house. "You're catch your death out there!"

Marti was confused by his reaction. Why would he care if she *caught her death*, as he put it? "I went by the station," she said, "but your sergeant told me you were gone for the day. I would not have bothered you at home except we really need to go over how we're going to handle my time within your department."

But then she sneezed again. And he seemed angry about that too. "Come here," he said to her and began walking away.

She wondered if she should close the front door since he didn't seem to care, but she didn't come from a place where she could leave doors opened or unlocked. She closed the door, locked it, sat her soaking wet briefcase on the floor in the foyer, and then hurried behind the chief.

She hated that she was dripping onto his hardwood floors, but he didn't seem to mind that either. So she continued to follow him down a long hall that led to a bathroom. "Get out of those clothes," he said to her as he grabbed a robe that was hanging on the bathroom door and tossed it at her. She caught it. "I'll run them through the dryer."

Then he opened the drawer from the fancy dressing table and grabbed a pair of unopened bootie socks and tossed them at her too. "Put these on. Those shoes are soaked through." Then he walked out of the bathroom and closed the door, with her inside.

She was so caught off guard that she didn't know what to make of this man. He was going to dry her clothes for her? It would have made more sense for them to just sit out on the porch, have their little meeting, and then send her on her way. And she was about to open that bathroom door and suggest that very thing.

But then she sneezed again. And she knew she had to get those wet clothes off of her.

It was unorthodox. It was stupid-crazy considering how she knew he felt about her and that anger she saw when he first opened his front door. But she got out of those clothes, anyway, feeling strange to be naked in that man's house. But when she thought about the position she was really in, she nearly fell on her face as she began putting on that robe so fast.

Then she smoothed her wet hair with a backward stroke of her hands, found a hair tie she always kept in her pocket, and put her hair into a thick ponytail. And then she just stood there, staring at herself in the mirror. What on earth was she doing? And even as she sneezed again, she wondered why did she agree to this? Was it because it was *him*? Was that really the reason? Did he pull her into his house because it was *her*? Was that really his reason?

She didn't know. But when she began to imagine him bursting through that bathroom door demanding something from her she wasn't willing to give to him, she hurried out of there.

CHAPTER ELEVEN

But as soon as she left the bathroom, she quickly returned and put on the clean socks she had forgotten to put on, and then she made her way back up front.

But she didn't see him anywhere. Just her luck, the chief of police might be a serial killer or some sadistic rapist who had her right where he wanted her. But she'd dealt with those kind of people her entire career. The worst of the worst. She didn't get that kind of vibe from him AT ALL. "Chief McGraw?" she called out.

"In here!"

She followed the sound of his voice through the living room, the massive dining hall, and all the way into the massive kitchen. If there was a theme in that house? It was huge. Everything was *huge*. Including, she recalled, the chief's penis.

Although she never once let it be known, she absolutely noticed when he had that erection and tented at his front door. It was like one of those *Damn! Already?* moments for her.

When she walked into the kitchen, he

was standing behind the huge center island pouring himself a glass of wine. With the sleeves rolled up on his sweatshirt, she could see how well-built he was. How attractive he was. "Where's the dryer?" she asked him.

He gulped down the shot of wine in his glass, sat the glass on the marbled countertop, and then walked around and took her clothes from her. The blouse and slacks she didn't mind, but she had no intention of allowing him to dry her bra and panties. She was going to put them in her briefcase until she got back to her hotel room. But he took those too.

"But Chief, I can dry my own clothes. You just need to tell me where."

But he was already walking to the laundry room that, she realized, was just off from the kitchen. And that was large too. He placed her clothes in what looked like a commercial-size dryer, putting them in one by one she noticed. Then he turned it on and walked back out into the kitchen.

"Have you eaten?" he asked as he began pouring her a glass of wine.

"I'm good," she said. All she wanted was to discuss the parameters of her assignment with him and then get out of Dodge.

Grant looked at her as he slid a glass of

wine toward her. "That's not what I asked you. Have you eaten?"

She didn't want to admit it. She wanted no favors from him. But she hadn't and she was starved. "No sir."

But then he noticed something seemingly on her forehead. She wondered what it was. Then he reached into a drawer beneath the center island, pulled out a blow-dryer and then walked around to Marti. But instead of handing the dryer to her, he plugged it in, removed her hair tie, and began blow-drying her hair himself. "It's still dripping," he said to her.

Was this man for real? It was like insanity to her. He was actually drying her clothes *and* her hair? It was weird on top of crazy to Marti. "I can dry it," she said to him, attempting to get control of the dryer.

"I know you can," he said to her, refusing to relinquish the blow-dryer. He continued to dry her hair until he was satisfied that her scalp, especially, was dry. Then he unplugged it, walked back around, and placed it back beneath the center island.

But when he looked at her again, he smiled for the first time since she met him.

"What's so funny?" she asked him.

"You look like Don King."

But what warmed Grant's heart was that Marti wasn't offended, nor did she hurry to the bathroom to spruce herself up. She actually smiled too. "The way you dried my hair with no consideration for styling it, I probably look more like Buckwheat," she joked, and they both laughed out loud.

"Probably so," he said.

And just like that the ice was broken.

As the chief went back to cooking his food, Marti took that opportunity to ask him about how he saw her role in his department.

"It depends on your goal."

"*My* goal?"

"Are you there to consult, or are you there to spy?" He glanced back at her.

"That's a fair question," she admitted. "I'm there to consult."

"And how will this consulting take place?"

"That's up to you."

"How do you envision it taking place?"

"Total cooperation. You make it clear to your employees that I'm there to help, not to harm them. That I'm there to review how they're operating and suggest ways that may produce better outcomes."

"We won't be arresting innocent people," said Grant as he glanced back at her again.

"In other words?"

"Right."

Grant turned his pot off: the stew was ready. But before he plated any food, he went back over to the center island and poured himself another glass of wine. "If I told you that a police department had a forty-nine percent exoneration rate on DNA samples taken from various arrests, what would you assume?"

Marti didn't skip a beat. "That the police department in question was poorly run."

That felt like a gut punch to Grant. "Why would you say that?"

"Why wouldn't I say it? Rot always starts from the inside out. And the inside man is always at the top."

Grant tried to smile. "You're calling my police department rotten?"

"I'm calling you rotten as the head of that police department," Marti made clear. "I've only been here two days and I've already seen that every member of the Belgrave Police Department follows your lead. Every one of them."

Grant studied her. "So I'm the problem?"

"You have a forty-nine percent DNA exoneration rate. If not you, then who?"

Grant was stunned by how candid she

was right in his face. Anybody else talked to him so bluntly and they would be the one with the problem. But he appreciated her bluntness. She wasn't the type to kiss his ass, and he respected that. But that didn't mean it didn't hurt.

But Marti was curious too. "How can you sleep at night with that kind of horrible result?"

He couldn't sleep at night even before the results came in. "I sleep good at night," he lied. Then added, echoing a commercial: "On Mattress Firm."

At first Marti was confused. Then she remembered the commercial, too, and laughed out loud.

He joined her. But even she could see that his joy didn't quite reach his eyes.

"Let's eat," he said as he proceeded to prepare two plates of food and told her to follow him into the dining hall. She grabbed her glass of wine and followed him.

They sat at the long table across from each other, in that massive dining hall, but it still felt intimate to Marti. She found that she liked him. He wasn't nearly as bad and closed-minded as she expected him to be. But she wondered if she had hurt his feelings regarding his horrific exoneration rate because he ate without saying another word to her.

"This is really good," she said to him. And she was not lying. "I'm not a particular fan of stew, but this tastes great."

He nodded his head and kept on eating.

"Who taught you how to cook so well?"

It was obvious he didn't like talking during his meals: there was something really formal about him. But he finished chewing and spoke. "Self-taught," he said. Then said nothing else.

When they finished eating, he finally spoke again. "I'll tell my men," he said, "to let you do your job."

Marti smiled. "I appreciate that. Thank you."

Then he pointed his fork at her. "But you stay out of their way, and my way, while you do it."

That sounded kind of harsh, but she was pleased to have his buy-in anyway. "I will," she agreed. But then she felt a need to add: "I didn't mean to hurt your feelings, Chief."

Grant frowned. "My *feelings*? What the hell does my feelings have to do with anything? Don't you dare apologize to me. I'm the chief of police and I'm lousy at it. That's just the truth. So don't you dare patronize me."

"I wasn't trying to patronize you."

"Show me how I can do a better job, and I'll do a better job. Isn't that why you're here?"

He could be a hard man. But Marti knew hard. That was the only kind of men she'd ever known. "Yes sir," she said.

Grant stared at her. He knew he'd hurt her feelings alright, and he regretted it. And if he was to be honest with himself, he was hurt by her bluntness too. But at least they understood each other. "If this marriage is going to work." A look of horror appeared on his face as soon as he said that word.

Even Marti was stunned. Marriage? Did he say *marriage*?

And he immediately caught himself. "Excuse me, if this *situation* is going to work, then we have got to keep it real. Beginning with no bullshit."

Marti recovered too. "On either side?"

Grant nodded. "On either side, that's correct."

Marti smiled. "I can live with that all day long. That'll work for me."

Grant liked her smile. She had dimples for one thing. And her smile seemed to unburden her for another thing. *Did anybody ever tell you how beautiful you are*? he wanted to ask her, but he wasn't about to do that. Because it was obvious she didn't like that kind of attention. Her hair was still uncombed and doing its own thing and she wasn't giving it a second thought. Which made him smile too. "You know you still look like Don King," he said to her.

And she laughed again. He adored her laugh. "That doesn't bother you?" he asked her.

She shook her head. "Not in the least. It is what it is. I'll take care of it when I can get to my hotel room and get what I need to do what I do. In the meantime bump it."

Grant had to know. That folder the mayor gave to him didn't mention her personal info. "How does your husband feel about your carefree attitude?"

Carefree? *Her*? Was he serious? She took a sip of her wine. "I'm divorced."

Grant was pleased to hear it. But how long ago mattered. "Recently?"

"Heavens no! Many, many, many years ago. He passed away after we divorced."

"Sorry to hear that. Was he a good man?"

Marti hesitated. "No."

Grant studied her. She'd been hurt more times than she'd probably ever admit. "Any kids?"

A look appeared in her massive eyes

that wasn't there before. A look Grant didn't recognize. She sipped more wine, but it felt like a shield to Grant. "No," she said. "No children."

Then she looked at him. "What about you? Any kids? Wife?"

A look appeared in his eyes that she thought she recognized. "I'm not married," he said, although it wasn't entirely her question.

But in that moment they found themselves staring at each other as if they were assessing each other. And suddenly their generally easy interaction felt uncomfortable and tense. As if there was bullshit between them. As if they weren't keeping it real. As if it was going to be as superficial a relationship as all their other acquaintances. And for Grant that was a shame. He liked their truthfulness with each other. He welcomed it. "Your clothes are ready."

It was only when he said it did Marti hear the buzz of the dryer finishing its run.

She quickly got up from his table, went into his laundry room, and closed the door behind her. She leaned against the door fighting back tears. It had been four years. Four years! And still just the mention of children drove her back to that awful place again. The running. The screams. The horror of it all.

She dressed quickly and hurried back out.

After retrieving her shoes from the bathroom, and smoothing her hair back down as best she could into a ponytail, she made her way toward the foyer. The chief was waiting for her there.

"I left your bathrobe in the laundry room," she said. "I'm sure you would want to wash it."

"Wash it why? Because you wore it ? Miss Nash, don't be ridiculous."

Marti smiled, which made him smile too. "Well. Thanks for dinner, and the blow-dry," she said, and Grant laughed.

"But please call me Marti."

"Not Markita?"

"Please no," she said, and he laughed at that too.

"Will do," he said.

"What's your hours of operation?" she asked him.

"Twenty-four hours. What are yours?"

"According to the AG's office, it's supposed to be ten to six with total flex."

"Then so be it. I'll see you tomorrow at ten."

That sounded great to Marti. She was bone tired. She could use a later wake up call. "Oh, before I forget," she said as she pulled a folder out of her still wet but no longer dripping briefcase. "These are my credentials." She handed him the folder. "I was supposed to give them to you on my arrival. Sorry."

He accepted them and opened his front door for her. "I'll see you tomorrow, Miss . . . I mean Marti," he said.

"And thanks again, Chief, for dinner." He waited for her to return her politeness and say that she could call him Grant. But such a curtesy wasn't extended to her. "It was very good," she added to save face.

He nodded, but it was a kind of frosty nod. The ice had melted, but it was still icy. Which made him moody. Which made him unreliable. Which made her curb the enthusiasm she was building for the chief. And then she left. She wasn't there to make friends anyway.

Grant walked over to his huge picture window as she made her way across his porch. The rain had stopped half an hour ago, but she still walked down those wet steps carefully, like she was a very cautious girl. And as she got into her Charger, he noticed how she still didn't bother about her hair when all the black women he'd ever been with obsessed over their hair. But she didn't give it a second glance. Didn't even look in her overhead mirror at all. She was a different kind of lady, he thought, as she drove away. He remained at the window and opened her file.

Eleven years as a cop, which surprised him. Made it to detective early in her career and all the way up the ranks to lieutenant. A police consultant was a decided downgrade for her.

Why the switch, he wondered.

And *marriage*? He still couldn't believe he said the word marriage. Where did that come from, he wondered even more.

CHAPTER TWELVE

"Man you're out of your mind. The Jaguars crushing the Dolphins? Get out of here!"

The senior staff were all in Grant's office going on and on about everything but police work when his desk phone buzzed. He picked it up. "What?"

"Marti Nash is here to see you, Chief."

Grant's heart squeezed as soon as his officer said her name. Feeling exposed, he quickly looked at the clock on the phone. It was twelve after ten. "Send her through," he said, and ended the call.

"Send who through?" RJ asked. "That consultant? My next meal?" They all laughed. All except for Grant.

"*Your* next meal? Says who? Get in line," said Pete. "I got first dibs on that nice slab of rib!"

"Not before me you don't," said another lieutenant.

"The chief told me to stay away from her," said RJ. "Chief got first."

"I don't have any such thing and neither do any of you," Grant shot back angrily.

"That's out of the question. For all of you. And I mean it."

"Sure Boss," said RJ very insincerely, and the guys all laughed at that too. Except for Grant.

And then knocks were heard on the Chief's office door.

"Enter!"

When that door opened and Marti walked in, those feelings deep inside of Grant came bubbling up once again. It felt as if his heart had just walked in, which was freaking him out inside. Why would he feel that way about that particular woman? *Why?*!

And she walked in looking so refreshed, he thought, with her thick hair now beautifully done in large curls down her back with plenty of bounce, and that same briefcase from last night by her side. She wore a belted pair of slacks with a blouse tucked in that perfectly highlighted her gorgeous body. When she walked in over half of the men in the room, including Grant, went hard. "You're late," he said, to cover it.

"I was out front on time," Marti made clear, "but your desk clerk had to get somebody to escort me back here. Then they had to call you first. Perhaps you can let them know that I have a right to be back here?"

"You have a *right*?" asked Lieutenant Pete. "Your rights are based on what rights we give you."

"Facts," echoed RJ.

Marti was so accustomed to good old boys in her line of work that she ignored them. Kept her eyes on the chief, whom she noticed didn't correct their disrespect. She was beginning to believe that he never bothered to correct anything they did because he pretty much let them do whatever the hell they wanted to do. He was a leader, she saw that two days ago at the Wafer House shooting. His men would follow him through the fire. But only if he asked them to. Grant McGraw, she believed, picked his battles very carefully. And his men showing her disrespect was no hill he was willing to die on. Which was fine by her. She could take care of herself.

When Grant stood up from behind his desk and grabbed a chair for her, she wasn't surprised when his men stood up too. They put on the show in front of him because they knew he would look the other way in other weightier matters. It was that kind of top-down police force.   And the top, if those men in that room were any indication, was rotten to the core.

Grant sat the chair beside his chair and

motioned for her to have a seat up front with him. When she walked up front next to him and he sniffed her sweet perfume scent, another level of arousal shot through his body. He held the chair as she sat down.

But when she sat down, his men remained standing, as if they wanted to make it clear to her that they weren't standing for her. When Grant sat back down behind his desk, his men sat down, too, to prove their point.

"I want to formally introduce you guys to our visitor, and I want you to notify your men of her arrival," Grant said to his principals after they all sat down. "As I'm sure you all know this young lady is Marti Nash, the police consultant from the office of the Attorney General of the great state of Florida."

Some of the men snickered. They knew what little regard Grant had for the AG's office and any other personnel in Chauncey Devere's corrupt administration.

"She's here to observe our policing practices from investigation to arrest, and we are required, as ordered by the Assistant AG himself, to allow her to do her job."

"When you say she'll observe us," said RJ, "what exactly does that mean?"

"Right," said Pete. "That's a wide-open criteria."

"Who's going to set the boundaries of what she can and cannot observe," added RJ, "because nobody wants to be spied on all day long?"

"She won't be spying on anybody," Grant said bluntly, "and I'll set the parameters of what she can observe."

That seemed to give them some comfort, Marti noticed.

"But," said Sergeant Carter, "this is going to seriously effect morale if it gets out of hand."

Grant was miffed. "What did I just say? Didn't I say I won't let it get out of hand?"

"Yes sir, but --"

"But what, Sergeant?"

Carter looked at RJ, their *other* leader and the only one in the room with the balls to stand up to their chief. "But it can go south real fast, Grant," said RJ. "That's what Sarge means. Cops don't like civilians coming in telling them how to do their jobs when they never walked a beat in their lives."

"Here here," said Pete. "That's what I'm talking about. What can she tell us? I was a cop before she was even born I'll bet, and many of our guys were too. But she's gonna tell us how to do *our* jobs?"

Marti looked to Grant to set those

buffoons straight, but he just sat there in what she realized up close was a very expensive suit, one of those Italian silk suits that no small-town police chief should be able to afford, and he allowed them to vent.

But what Marti didn't know was that he allowed them to vent so that he could see what she was made of. If she would defend herself. If she had the mettle to stand up to the alpha males on his police force, or if she was a weakling and he would have to hold her hand to protect her from the big, bad cops.

He leaned back in his chair and watched her as those big, bad cops gave him an earful.

"Will she follow us on our lunch breaks?"

"Will she sit in on interrogations of suspects?"

"Will she listen in on our private conversations?"

"Will we be ordered to allow her to hang around our houses after work the way she was hanging around yours last night?"

Grant frowned when Pete mentioned last night. "How would you know who was hanging around my house last night?" he asked him.

Pete realized he had said too much and looked to RJ to bail him out.

"What he meant was," RJ began saying,

but Grant cut him off.

"I don't give a damn what he meant." Grant's eyes remained on Pete. "How would you know who was hanging around my house last night?" he asked him again.

"It's my understanding that a beat cop drove by your house on his normal patrols and saw her car in your driveway."

Grant knew that was a lie because no beat cop patrolled his street. Especially since, given his acreage, his house was the only house within a mile on that street.

And although Grant was willing to let it slide since they had real police work to get to, Marti wasn't about to. Her reputation mattered to her and no bozos from Belgrave were going to trample on it as if she was some hoe in town ready for whatever *hoedown* they threw her way. "I was at the chief's house last night," she said, addressing Pete directly, "because your sergeant gave me his address and told me he would love to meet with me at his house."

RJ smiled and then laughed, prompting all of the other senior staff to laugh. Marti was offended. "Did I say something funny?"

"Everybody knows that Chief Grant McGraw does not allow any human being inside his house," RJ said.

"He doesn't allow dogs and cats in there

either," Pete added, and they all laughed at that.

Marti glanced at Grant. He didn't allow anybody to go inside his house, but yet he all but pulled her inside of that same house and washed her clothes for her and even blow-dried her hair? No man had ever even thought about doing something like that for her. And he allowed her to have dinner with him too? A man who never wanted company? That sounded crazy to Marti. That made no sense to her. Why would he be so kind to her if he shunned all others?

But his kindness toward her was none of their business. "I didn't know anything about that," was all she said about her visit to his house, and she pivoted back to the point. "When you assumed that I've never been a beat cop, your assumption is absolutely wrong."

"Why's that?" asked Pete. "You were a cop for a few days, maybe even a few months, and couldn't cut the muster? And because of that nothing service we're supposed to give you street cred?"

"She doesn't need you to give her shit," said Grant. "She was a detective lieutenant with the Memphis Police Department. She's no 90-day wonder. She's an eleven-year veteran cop from a jurisdiction that will make ours look like shitsville."

When he said those words, the gasps in the room made Marti inwardly smile. It was as if they couldn't believe it.

Because they couldn't. "I thought that consultant stuff was the job for slobs who couldn't cut it as cops," said Sergeant Carter.

"Or some college nerd that never was a cop," said another senior staff in the room.

"Why would a veteran police officer want to be a *consultant*?" asked RJ. And he said it as if the very word itself was a contaminant.

"Isn't that like a super-major downgrade?" asked Carter.

"Why would you walk away from being a lieutenant to becoming some nothing consultant?" asked Pete. "That's like Gladys Knight deciding to become a Pip." They all laughed.

Grant looked at Marti. He was curious too.

But she said nothing about it. He could tell their questions rattled her. He saw it by the way she sat upright in her seat as if she needed to stiffen her backbone. But she, instead, moved on. "I won't be observing anything personal," she said to the men. "That's not my job. I'm here only to take a closer look at the techniques you guys are using and why those techniques might have led to your extremely high DNA exoneration rate. That's my one and only focus. There are just too many innocent people being arrested, tried and convicted in this jurisdiction. Why is that?"

"Ask the State Attorney's office. They're the ones with the final say on who gets prosecuted. Not us," said RJ.

"Right," agreed Pete and the rest of the senior staff.

"It's true that the State Attorney's office decides who gets prosecuted," said Marti. "But it's based completely on the evidence that you present to them. It begins with you. Something is wrong at the beginning of the process, not the middle of it. It's my job to find out what's wrong in the beginning."

The seniors looked at each other. Marti could tell they didn't like it one bit. But that wasn't her problem.

"Anything else?" Grant asked, rescuing her.

"We're good," said RJ, although Marti could tell they weren't satisfied at all.

"Alright everybody back to work," Grant announced, and the men stood up to leave.

"What do we call you?" one of the

lieutenants asked.

"Everybody calls me Marti."

"You will call her Lieutenant Nash," Grant ordered. He knew his men. Give'em an inch, and they'd take a mile. The men left, closing the door behind them.

"If any one of my men call you Marti or anything other than Lieutenant, you correct them. That's the only way you'll get any respect out of them."

Marti looked at Grant. He said nothing while they grilled her, but now he was concerned about them respecting her? And based on some title she no longer even had? This man was becoming a serious enigma to her!

"About that Wafer House shooting," she said. "How's the investigation going? Have you found the gunman yet?"

"Not yet, no."

"Do you have any leads?"

"None. We let the bad guy get away because we had eyewitnesses that pointed us in a different direction. We're investigating those eyewitnesses."

Marti knew that was a waste of time. They had faulty memories because of the trauma, not because they were intentionally lying. But any cop should have known that.

"Last night I reviewed in detail the demographics for this police department because I noticed something that I had to confirm with data."

While Grant was reviewing her credentials, she was apparently reviewing his department. "What did you notice?"

"I noticed, and the data confirms, that there are no women on your police force."

Grant studied her. "There are women."

"In dispatch roles, yes, but not as police officers."

"This is a very conservative town. Men aren't too keen on their wives in the line of fire."

"Blacks aren't keen on blacks in the line of fire either?"

What was she talking about? "Say again?" asked Grant.

"I also noticed that in a town that has a nearly forty-one percent African American population, there's only one black guy on the entire police force. Just one. And that's if you can call him black."

Grant had her a hard look. Was she one of those bleeding-heart liberals that viewed everybody else as weird and wrong? "What do you mean if you can call him black?"

"Just what I said."

"If he's not black, then what is he?"

"He's an oreo. Which is his right. He can be whatever he wants to be. But he's it. The black population, essentially, has no representation on this police force whatsoever. That's a problem."

"What's an oreo? Other than a cookie?"

Marti sometimes forgot that she wasn't in Memphis anymore. "A person black on the outside, but white on the inside. A sellout. An Uncle Tom. Whatever you choose to call them. But that's his right."

"And why would having one black man, and a very high-ranking one at that, be a problem?"

"Because sixty-five percent of the prisoners that were at least technically exonerated by DNA were African American. That's why."

Grant stared at her. "What's your solution if it's such a problem you're making it out to be?"

Marti didn't like the premise of his question, but she picked her battles too. "Fire some of these good old boy rednecks and hire more African Americans."

The desk intercom buzzed before Grant could respond. Grant pressed the button. "The mayor's office just called, sir."

"And?"

"He wants you and that lady--"

"*That lady* is Lieutenant Nash," Grant corrected his desk clerk.

"Excuse me, sir. That's the way the mayor referred to her."

Grant glanced at Marti. "What does he want?"

"He wants you and the lieutenant in his office right now."

"Did he say what for?"

"No sir. But he's upset."

Grant ended the conversation and just sat there, seemingly taking his own counsel, Marti thought. Then he stood up, prompting Marti to stand too. He grabbed his suitcoat off of the back of his chair. "Let's go," he said, and began hurrying for the exit.

Marti grabbed her briefcase and followed him. He knew the mayor was the chief's boss, but she had a feeling that wasn't why he would have hurried out. The mayor, apparently, rarely called him over to City Hall. And he was upset too? Something was up, and it wasn't something good, was how Marti interpreted it.

But as the twosome made their way through the lobby to the exit doors, RJ, Pete, and Carter were leaned against the information desk watching them leave. They noticed how the chief opened the door for the consultant and then placed his hand on her lower back as they walked out of the station. The three men also noticed, as they walked over to the front window, how their chief opened the passenger door of his Mercedes for her and did something they found quite intimate: he buckled her in.

"How you like that?" asked Pete. "He's scaring us away from her so he could have it all for himself."

"You think he's tapping that already?" asked Carter.

"Hell yeah," said Pete.

But it was RJ, who was actually in the know around there, that Carter wanted to hear it from. "You think so, too, Cap?"

"Grant McGraw has never met a woman he hasn't slept with." RJ looked at Carter. "So what do you think?"

Carter grinned. "Chief twenty years older than I am and he gets more action than I get! That's not fair," he added and laughed.

But as they watched the chief and Marti drive away, RJ and Pete were far more serious. "What do we do, Cap?" Pete asked as they watched.

"Tell them to get ready. Her presence could be a serious problem. We may have to move sooner than planned."

Pete exhaled. "If this don't work, we are screwed," Pete said. "You know that right?"

"What do you mean *we*, white man?" asked RJ.

Pete and Carter looked at him. Sometimes they wondered if they were being played by him and if this black man really was one of them. But then he plastered on that smile that always reassured them, and all their doubts flew away. And they smiled too.

"Stop worrying," RJ said. "Nobody's getting screwed. Except the chief, of course," he added, and they all laughed.

But RJ knew it could all blow up in their faces. He knew they were taking a hell of a risk.

CHAPTER THIRTEEN

City Hall, with its tall white pillars and brick colonial architecture, reminded Marti of Grant's enormous house when they drove into the slanted parking space. Marti moved to get out, but the door remained locked and could only be unlocked by Grant. But he was just sitting there.

Then he looked over at her. According to her credentials she was thirty-seven years old, and although she looked every bit of her age, if not older, those years gave her a maturity about her, a sophistication, that he found appealing. He fooled around with women of all ages, but lately he'd been messing with women in their twenties who knew how to bring it in bed but exhausted him otherwise. The neediness. They clinginess that he didn't tolerate. The greed. It was all getting to be too much. He wondered if her independence was his attraction to her. Her toughness. Her bluntness. The fact that she could take care of herself. Qualities in a woman he had grown unaccustomed to seeing. Qualities that always turned him on.

But not just that. *She* turned him on.

The way her natural eyelashes curved down around her large eyes that gave her a look so sexy that Grant often found himself staring at her. But what was even sexier to him was that unlike every woman he'd ever been with, she didn't seem to realize the effect she had on men. Or on *him*. "Mayor Rickter is an asshole," he said to her. "Just so you know."

Marti smiled. "If I had a dollar for every asshole I've been around, I'd be a rich girl."

Grant smiled too, something he rarely did. "Just so you know," he said, unbuckled, and opened the door.

Marti started to protest that he needed to unlock her door since he apparently had it set that way in his car's computer, but then she saw him walking around to the passenger side of his car and she decided to let him do his thing. He didn't come across to her as the kind of man that would bother to open car doors for ladies, but he did so at the station and was doing so at City Hall. He was opening doors for her. This after he had literally left her in the dust the first time they met. But that was Chief McGraw. He was like a rollercoaster ride. Up and down with him.

He opened her car door, she thanked him as she got out, and they made their way across the sidewalk to the front entrance. But when they were about to enter City Hall's revolving doors, and he stepped aside to let her enter first, he once again placed his hand on her lower back: something she recalled him doing at the station. It gave her a tingle when he touched her like that, but she pretended she didn't notice. Her purpose there was singular and she wasn't going to let some gruffy, moody police chief sidetrack her.

They entered the building and made their way onto the elevator. On the elevator, Marti noticed how Grant moved to the back while she stood up front. And although three other people were riding up with them, she could feel his stare. When the elevator dinged just before the doors slid open, she quickly glanced back and confirmed her suspicion: She caught him staring at her butt.

Grant's eyes did not behave as if he cared that she caught him assessing her body. He even looked up into her eyes. When their eyes met, it was Marti who seemed caught off guard. It was Marti who hadn't been with a man in so long that the very idea of it terrified her. It was Marti who couldn't wait to get off of that elevator.

To make matters worse, when they did step off of the elevator on the top floor, a beautiful woman was about to get on. Until she saw the chief.

"Grant!" She seemed taken aback to see him. "What are you doing here?"

"Meeting with Dooney. What are you doing here?"

"Meeting with the budget director about the Ball. You haven't returned my calls." Then she glanced over at Marti. "I was wondering why. Am I on the outs again? And if so, who's in?"

Marti could hear Grant sneer. "That's none of your business," he said to the woman.

She actually smiled, although Marti could tell she was also pissed. "Same old Grant. The big news is which lady are you taking to the Ball this year." She glanced at Marti again. "I've never known you to go for the Cinderella type."

Grant's jaw tightened when she took that swipe at Marti. "Apparently I do," he said. "I took you one year, didn't I?"

Marti couldn't suppress her smile, and didn't try to. The woman tried to laugh it off herself, but her eyes gave her away. "I'm still waiting for my ask," she had the nerve to say.

"Keep waiting," Grant said, placed his arm on Marti's lower back again, and escorted her away from the elevator. When Marti glanced back, the woman was staring hate daggers. But not at Grant, but seemingly at Marti!

"That woman looks like she wants to kill me," Marti said to him as they walked away.

Grant didn't bother to look at her again. "She knows the rules," he said, his hand pressing harder against Marti's slender back when he said it.

But Marti wanted to know what rules he was talking about. Did he mean that he and that woman had an open relationship with no attachments? With no commitments? Or was it a private relationship and they were supposed to have no public displays? She wanted to ask him all those questions, but she knew he would tell her it was none of her business just like he told that woman. And he'd be absolutely right. She said nothing.

They made it to the Mayor's office and were told that they could go right in.

Dooney Rickter was seated behind his desk and didn't bother to stand up when they walked in. He didn't even bother to look away from the computer screen in which he was staring.

"Sit down," he said to both of them.

Marti moved to sit down, but Grant pulled her back up. "You haven't been formally introduced."

Dooney looked up at him. "Who says I wanna be?"

"Mayor Rickter, this is Lieutenant Nash, our consultant."

"*Our* consultant? You mean Chauncey Devere's consultant. I know what that governor of ours is up to. She's more like our spy."

"I don't spy for anyone," Marti corrected the mayor.

He gave Marti a nasty look. Then he gave her that assessing look-over. "Tell me this, Miss Nash, how many sleepovers did you have with Chauncey to get this gig?"

To Marti's shock, Grant angrily reached over that desk, grabbed the mayor by his suitcoat, and pulled him up until they were face to face. Marti could tell the mayor was shocked too. So much so that he didn't have the words to say.

"Watch it, Dooney," Grant warned him.

But even Grant was surprised by his own actions. He released the mayor.

The mayor straightened his suitcoat angrily, and for some reason he looked over at Marti as if it was all her fault. But Marti was still reeling from Grant's reaction to the mayor's putdown of her. It had been a long time, too long to even remember how long it had been, since anybody stood up for her. And to the mayor no less? This man Grant McGraw continued to amaze and baffle and infuriate her all at the same time.

"Have a seat," the mayor said to them again.

"Apologize to the Lieutenant."

"I'm not going to--"

"*Apologize*!" Grant said it so angrily that it made the mayor wince. "You will not ever disrespect this lady as if she's some low-grade slut, and expect no retribution. Because you will get it."

"From you?"

"You better believe it."

"Why?" the now-confused mayor asked his police chief. "Since when did you care about some female?"

But it was a question Grant couldn't answer. And didn't try to answer.

"I could fire you," the mayor said to Grant. "You know that?"

"You'd better apologize to her. I know that."

The mayor's anger flared. "Who do you think you are talking to me like that? Are you out of your *got*damn mind?"

Sometimes Grant wondered if he had a screw loose. Why else was he so offended by some jerk like Dooney Rickter disrespecting a woman he barely knew? He'd never gotten that heated for women he knew for years. But for this one he was all bothered under the collar? It made no sense! But Dooney still was going to apologize. Grant was not allowing that level of disrespect against Marti to stand. Not that level.

Somehow Mayor Rickter knew it too. "If I offended you," he said to Marti, "I apologize."

Marti and Grant both knew it was an apology erroneously couched in an *I believe everything I said to you, but if you didn't like it then I'll say the words you want to hear to put an end to it* excuse. But it was better than nothing.

"No worries," Marti said.

Then the mayor, once again, invited them to sit down. This time, they sat down.

Dooney sat down too. "It leaked," he said as soon as his butt hit the chair.

Grant instantaneously knew what he meant. Marti had a good guess.

"What's the fallout?" Grant asked him.

The mayor leaned back in his chair. "They want you gone," he said.

"That's nothing new," Grant said. "You never wanted me in the role anyway."

"Damn right I didn't."

"Did you leak it?"

"Fuck you, McGraw! Like I'm gonna leak that shit that'll take me down right along with you. We've gotta contain it."

"How?" asked Grant. "We've got a mass casualty shooter still on the loose. We've got more DVs than any other police department in this entire region."

"And we've got Governor Devere's spy in our midst!"

"I'm nobody's spy, Mayor Rickter," Marti corrected the mayor. "I don't do that."

"Then what are you here for?"

"To review the issues in this department and see what tools could be used to correct them."

Dooney smiled. "Whatever floats your boat." Then he looked at Grant. "Touch me again and I'll fire you."

"Then fire me," Grant responded. "You think I enjoy this shit?"

That was news to Marti, although she didn't know why it would be considering how poorly run that police department was. But it did surprise her.

Dooney looked at his chief. "It'll be my pleasure," he said to him, "but the BOBs won't allow it. You're their horse and they're riding with you all the way until they destroy me."

Marti noticed a theme with the mayor: It was always all about him. And who on earth were the BOBs?

"There's a press conference Friday," he said as Grant's phone began ringing. "I expect you to be there."

Grant looked at the Caller ID.

"I'm not going through that fire by myself," Dooney added.

But Grant answered the call. "What?" Then he frowned. "Are you serious? Where?" Then he jumped up. "All available units over there now! I'm on my way."

Marti jumped up too.

"Now what?" the mayor asked him.

"Another mass shooting," Grant said as he began hurrying for the exit. Marti hurried behind him.

The mayor was floored. "Not another one! Where?"

"Near here. Karney's," Grant said as he placed his hand on Marti's back and hurried her out of the office.

They raced for the elevator.

CHAPTER FOURTEEN

Karney's, it turned out, was a major grocery store in Belgrave that Marti had once drove by when she first arrived in town. Although two patrol cars were already on the scene by the time the chief sped his Mercedes into the parking lot, but those cars and all four officers were across the street from the parking lot using their cars for cover and with their guns drawn. But gunshots could be heard, even in that moment, inside the store.

Grant couldn't believe it. Marti couldn't either. "What are they doing?" she asked, looking at the officers. "Why haven't they gone inside?"

"That's what I wanna know," Grant said as they quickly got out of his car.

"Why aren't you in?" Grant yelled at his men as he hurried to the trunk of his car.

"We were waiting for instructions, sir," one of the patrolmen said.

"You hear gunfire you go and stop it," Marti yelled at them. "Those are the instructions! What are you talking about?"

But Marti also noticed that Grant didn't get on their case.

And that was by design. All four patrolmen were young, none with over a few years' experience, and mass shootings wasn't something they were accustomed to. Belgrave, in fact, had never had any mass shootings until this week. He grabbed his assault rifle from his trunk and ordered Marti to wait there. "And I mean wait here!" he ordered her.

Then he looked at his men. "Let's go," he said and they didn't hesitate. They ran along the side of the store, their guns drawn and ready. Like Marti truly believed, his men would run through the fire for him if he told them to. They all moved to the store's front entrance and, with Grant leading the way, they ran inside of the hot crime scene.

But when she saw Grant leading the charge, she felt a sudden pain shoot through her body. And she was suddenly frightened for him. That was why she decided to disregard his order, pulled out her own gun, and ran around the back.

She could tell that most of the gunfire was coming from the back of the store and if she could get in back and Grant and his men were up front, then that could create a critical mass that would force the gunman into the middle of gunfire from both directions. She was also betting that the back of the store was open because on police radio, as they were traveling to the scene, it was mentioned that many of the employees and customers had fled to the hardware store next door when the gunman first arrived. Which, for a man seeking to kill as many people in as fast a time as possible, would have meant he went in through the front. Which, following her logic, the customers and employees fled through the back. She was willing to bet that none of them bothered to close the door as they fled.

She realized she was right when she saw the back door wide open. And she didn't hesitate. She ran in as fast as she could. Her entire focus was to save as many people as she possibly could. And Grant, too, while she was at it.

As soon as she ran inside, she could see the gunman on the far right aisle running toward the front exchanging gunfire with Grant and his men. She ran to the far left aisle and followed his movements, her gun ready to fire.

But just as the gunman stopped running and began firing on Grant and his men, and just as she was about to give away her position and fire on him, she noticed another gunman that was locked and loaded and ready to ambush Grant and his men from the back. She knew then she had to forget about the first gunman and take out the second gunman, the ambusher, before he took out Grant.

Problem was she hadn't fired her weapon in four long years. Not since that night on her patio.

And as she ran as fast as she could to get an angle for her shot, and as soon as the second gunman stopped for his ambush attack, and was aimed and ready to fire on Grant and his men, Marti froze for a second. A flashback flew across her vision, of her standing on her patio firing shot after shot into Andy Sloan. And, *by extension*, into her own child.

What if she missed?

What if she hit another innocent bystander?

But what if that gunman shot and killed Grant McGraw?

123

And it was that *what if* that steeled her resolve, controlled her hammering heart, and she stopped hesitating and fired on that gunman in rapid succession. She nearly emptied her weapon firing on him.

And as soon as Marti's shots were fired at the second gunman, taking him out, the first gunman looked over in shock and turned his weapon on Marti. But Grant took full advantage of his sudden distraction and fired on him. Grant was an excellent shot. The first gunman fell too.

"Don't fire!" Marti yelled out to Grant's cops when they turned to fire on whomever was shooting in the back. "It's me, Marti Nash. The consultant! Don't shoot!"

But two of those patrolmen fired on her anyway, causing her to hit the floor.

Grant was pissed. "Didn't you hear her?" he yelled at his men. "Stop shooting!" He angrily pushed both trigger-happy men aside as he ran toward the far left aisle. Then he frantically called out for Marti. "Marti?" he yelled out. "*Marti*?!"

"I'm okay!" Marti yelled back when she heard the panic in the chief's voice. But when he appeared on her aisle, she felt nothing but relief. She was on the floor, but only because she hit the deck because she assumed his men, nervous and green, would shoot anyway. That was why they missed. She didn't take any chances. "Make sure the store is clear!" she yelled to Grant. "Make sure there are no more gunmen!"

"Check the store!" Grant yelled to his men, they yelled *yes, sir*, and Grant hurried to Marti. He was more concerned about her than anybody else in that store, especially when he saw her on the floor.

"Were you hit?" he asked her anxiously as he knelt down to her. More cops were running into the store as even more sirens could be heard arriving too. They had full backup now.

Marti sat up on her butt. "I wasn't hit. I got down because I assumed incoming was heading my way."

"Why would you make that assumption?" Grant was looking over her body to satisfy himself that she was okay. "Because of how poorly run this department is?"

Marti looked him in his beautiful, but anguished blue eyes. "Yes," she said without batting an eye. "No bullshit, right?"

He exhaled. He'd never met anybody like her. Then he nodded his head. And helped her to her feet.

Marti appreciated that he was not a

125

defensive man.

He wasn't an emotional man either. But when she got on her feet, he couldn't help himself. He pulled her into his arms.

Some of his men saw the chief hugging her, and she saw them elbow each other, and she knew it was highly inappropriate, but her heart was hammering. She was still shaking. She could have easily missed her target and became the target herself. For those reasons, when Grant pulled her into his arms, she allowed it. It became the first time anyone had held her in years. She *needed* it.

Grant needed it too. Because his heart was hammering even harder than hers. He thought she had been hit. He thought one of his dumb-ass guys had surely taken her out. But when he realized she was okay, he couldn't help it. He had to hold her. He just had to.

But when he heard RJ's voice up front, and he knew his senior people had arrived, he ended the embrace. He didn't want them thinking for a second that she was some easy tart they could try their luck with too.

But when he and Marti pulled apart, and looked into each other's eyes, a sweet, warm feeling overtook them both. And Grant actually smiled, with those lines of age beginning to appear around his eyes, and he squeezed her arm. "I'm glad you're okay," he said to her.

Marti smiled, too, and touched his arm. "Glad you are as well," she said.

It was awkward, because neither one of them were touchy-feely people, but for that same reason it was powerful too. It was no breakthrough. Neither one of them were trying to do anything more than be pleased that they both got out of that shooting alive, but it did feel different. Even great.

But then RJ and Pete Kerrigan showed up and Grant was pulled away to speak with several witnesses at the hardware store next door. But not before he fired on the spot both of the cops that didn't heed Marti's call out, and they shot at her anyway.

"I want you both as far away from my police department as you can get!" he yelled at the two men. "She announced who she was and you shot at her anyway? You're fired! Both of you. You're fired!"

Although Marti knew she could follow Grant to question the witnesses, she was never big on eyewitness accounts. She, instead, wanted to see the video footage. She hurried to the store manager's office where the monitors were housed. But Pete Kerrigan blocked her access. "Chief has to give permission," he said.

"No he doesn't," Marti said and dared him to say otherwise.

When he didn't take her dare, she remained in the video room, too, and watched the footage with Kerrigan, two other detectives, and the store manager. They knew who did it, but Marti wanted to know how. That way, if another mass shooting ever occurred, Grant and his department would have more information on how it worked. She saw the first gunman walked in and started shooting almost immediately. But she realized the second shooter was already inside the store, pretending to be a customer.

"There he is," she said and Pete and the manager looked closer.

They realized the second gunman had hid in the office that a lot of the customers ran into. And that was when he pulled out his weapon and took them all out. It would not have been a mass casualty event, but for that second gunman in that confined office setting, shooting everybody in his wake. As if, to Marti, the person they came to kill was in that office. A premeditated personal murder, perhaps, masquerading as a mass shooting? It was gruesome to see.

But after the video, she mostly

observed. Most of the guys she walked up on were talking more about their sexual exploits than any police work, until they realized she was near. Then the focus shifted entirely to police work. But nothing deep. They didn't seem to know anything deep. It was a telling indictment.

But she continued to move around. She would see the chief occasionally, but the mayor and the press showed up and he had to cater to them. So she was once again on her own. But the fact that he had held her, and that she liked that feeling he gave to her, weighed heavily on her mind. She wasn't ready to go down a road like that. Or was she? The fact that it wasn't clear to her anymore was what alarmed her.

"It's been a long day."

RJ walked over to Marti as she leaned against the chief's car in the cordoned off street waiting for him to come outside too. By now it was almost six pm.

"It's been a long day," RJ said again when he made it over to Marti.

"A very long day," Marti said. "Captain Jeffers, right?"

RJ plastered on that fake smile he was famous for, although very few people saw it for what it was. Marti saw it for what it was. "At your service," he said with a bow. "How did you know? Chief McGraw introduced you to us, but he didn't introduce us to you."

"Let's just say you stand out in the crowd," Marti said, and RJ laughed.

"I feel you sister. I most certainly feel you. But listen: Chief told me to give you a ride to your hotel room. He said he'll be here for hours more."

Marti would have expected the chief to dismiss her himself, but the fact that he couldn't take the time out to do it himself managed to bring her back to earth. That was why she knew better than to get her hopes up. That was why she knew not to put any stock whatsoever in that embrace. It was an *in the moment* reaction and nothing more. And why would Captain Jeffers offer to take her to her hotel, but not to the police station to pick up her car? Which would have made more practical sense.

But she was there to get intel on what exactly was wrong with the department. Captain Jeffers was an inside source. She could catch an Uber to work in the morning and get her car then. It would be in her per diem. And given the men she was dealing with, it just might be her only chance to get any inside information. "Thanks," she said, and gladly got into the unmarked police car he was driving.

But less than fifteen minutes later, after they had gone, Grant came outside looking for Marti. He was shocked to hear that she had already gone.

Without saying goodbye? he thought. "She's already gone?" he asked.

"About fifteen minutes ago, yes, sir," Pete said. But when he added, "RJ gave her a ride to her hotel," Grant's anger flared, he hopped into his car, and he sped away.

A detective, who was standing nearby, walked over to Pete smiling. "What was that all about, Lieutenant Pete?"

"If I didn't know any better," Pete replied, "I'd say our chief is smitten."

"Chief McGraw? With all those females he fools around with? And smitten with some consultant? Give me a break!"

But Pete held firm. He'd been on the force almost as long as that detective had been alive. And the chief giving a damn that one of his men might actually sleep with that consultant was not the chief he knew. Not by a longshot. Not by fifty miles.

Besides, Pete was hopeful. Because he knew, if RJ got some, he was going to get some eventually too. That was how it worked at the senior levels of the Belgrave PD. They had no problem passing their side pieces around, although, Pete inwardly knew, their chief had never passed anyone around. He would have to go, like he knew RJ was going, behind the chief's back.

"Enough about the chief," Pete finally said. "Let's wrap this shit up and go home. Both perps are dead. What the hell are we still hanging around here for?"

"Something they call police investigation perhaps," the detective jokingly said.

"Police investigation?" asked Pete. "What's that?"

And both men laughed.

CHAPTER FIFTEEN

"May I ask you a question?"

"You may ask me anything you like sweetheart." RJ drove through the streets of Belgrave with intent on his mind. When he heard that she was at the chief's house last night when the chief wouldn't even allow his own men to come anywhere near that precious house of his, he knew then he wasn't delaying any longer. He was getting his. "As long as it's not about me," he added, chuckling.

Marti smiled, too, although she viewed him as the leader of the department's good old boys' network. But she needed info and saw him, a true insider, as her best opportunity. The little she knew about Captain Jeffers, based on bits and pieces of conversations she'd heard while walking around observing all day, was that he was married to a white woman, had kids, and slept around as if he was the most eligible bachelor in town.

And it wasn't just him. Everybody on that force appeared to be just like him, from what she was hearing. Including the chief – she was willing to bet. Although they didn't say much about the chief. But that was probably because he kept his private life private, while his men were plotting and planning their latest escapades even as they worked on a horrific crime scene. "Just general questions," she said to RJ.

"Then ask away."

"Why hasn't the chief hired more African Americans on the force?"

"Ah." He nodded his head. "Or women, right?"

"Right."

"He would hire them all day long if it was left up to him. He's that kind of dude. But he can't. He doesn't do the hiring."

That was news to Marti. "Then who does?"

"The members of the Belgrave Oversight Board. The *BOBs* as we call them. They do all the hiring. Grant can fire at will. He wouldn't take the job without that particular power, although I've yet to see him use it until today."

This interested Marti. "He's never fired anyone before today?"

"Never. And there's been tons of times he should have used that power, in my humble opinion. But when they shot at you? Oh no. They had to go then. He got rid of those jokers right on the spot." He laughed and looked at

Marti. "You must have that special sauce girl."

Marti ignored his flirtatiousness. "Why would he agree to let some board dictate who'll be on his police force though?"

"It was out of his hands. The chief before him did his own hiring. But he was hiring a bunch of Klan members who acted as if they were his personal vendetta squad, and he hired drug dealers that gave him kickbacks from their illicit trade. And I'm talking hardcore drug people. The kind of people you wouldn't hire to mow your lawn, let alone police your city. They fired that chief before the FBI got called in, and then the city took the hiring power out of the hands of any future chief. They passed a referendum that a board of citizens would do all the hiring in the police department. And the Belgrave Oversight Board, or BOB, was created. And they can overrule any firing the chief does too. So stay tuned," he said with a smile.

Marti shook her head. "Wow. That's a lot of power invested in one board."

"They love it. They're the city's power brokers."

"But who are they exactly?"

"A bunch of rich white guys just like the chief."

Marti looked at RJ. Because that was

her main question. Was the chief rich organically, or because of corruption? That was what Marti needed to know. "I was wondering how a police chief in a town this size could afford to drive around in a Maybach."

"Oh he's rich. A Maybach ain't no big deal to Grant McGraw. So get that out of your pretty little head."

Marti didn't know how to take that comment. Was he assuming her to be interested in the chief? "Get what out of my head?"

"Corruption," said RJ. "Grant is a lot of things, but he's no crooked cop. Can't nobody buy him. He can buy this whole town if he wanted to, but can't nobody buy him. He made millions in the tech industry out in California. But something happened and he sold his company and moved back home. Belgrave is his hometown. Mine too."

"What happened? Why did he sell his company and come back home?"

"Nobody knows. He doesn't talk about it and I'm sure you've already figured out that you don't just go up to Grant McGraw and ask him personal stuff like that. But he's been back for eight years now, and he's been chief for six."

Interesting, Marti thought. Then she had another thought. What does his men think of his leadership? "Is he a good cop?" she asked RJ.

RJ hesitated on that question. "He tends to run the police force like he probably ran his tech company. He gives out assignments and expect his men to get it done. Does he hold their hands and make them do it right? No. Does he check to make sure they did it right? No. That's my job and the other senior staff. He delegates. That's what he does."

"And that's why you have a horrible exoneration rate."

RJ nodded. "I can't disagree with you there. He's good peeps. Don't get me wrong. But he's checked out too."

"Since when?"

"Since he been here. He's never checked in if you ask me. But he's no crooked cop if that's what you're fishing for. And he doesn't tolerate it either."

For some reason, Marti was pleased to hear it. He wasn't some backwater cop who didn't give a damn, but a man of depth. She'd never admit it publicly, but she liked Chief McGraw. He was gruff and hard around the edges for sure, but to Marti there was a decency, an elegance about him that elevated him from your run-of-the-mill copper. She'd already seen that.

But if RJ was right, the man she *liked* was also a millionaire when she had assumed he owned that big house and fancy car because he was on the take. It made her feel kind of intimidated if she was to tell herself the truth. She'd never been around a man with big money like that. She'd never had dinner with one, never had one dry her clothes – including her panties! Never had one blow-dry her hair or defend her honor when the mayor of this town all but called her a slut. Or hugged her in a grocery store when she needed a hug.

But hearing RJ made her realize just how amazing their chief might actually be. Because, in truth, no man had ever treated her as well as Grant McGraw treated her. Not even her ex-husband when they were still in love. Or at least when *she* was still in love. She found out love was never on his agenda. Just lust and *bragging rights* as he called them. But those were the kind of men, throughout her life, she gravitated to. Never one like the chief.

RJ glanced over at her. "We've been talking a lot about the chief," he said. "What about you?"

"What about me?"

"I heard the AG isn't paying those consultants much money at all. Like just above minimum wage or something like that."

"And?"

"*And* why would an accomplished sister like you want a thankless, nothing job like that? Why aren't you still a cop?"

"Not interested any longer."

"Why not?"

She wasn't about to tell her life story to a man who didn't want to get into her heart, but into her panties. "No longer interested."

RJ nodded his head. She could dish it, but she couldn't take it. She was happy to put everybody else under the microscope, but not her own damn self. But he had a cure for that. One round with him and she'd be confessing all night long. It never failed.

"We're here," he said as he turned another corner and drove into the parking lot of the Hilton Garden Inn hotel. "I'll walk you up," he added as he got out and then hurried around and opened the car door for her. Which made her inwardly smile. If he thought she was going to give it up to some married man, he had the wrong sister. But with a good-looking brother like Captain Jeffers, who was probably accustomed to getting his way with women, she knew she had to show it rather than tell it. She allowed him to escort her up to her hotel room.

But once they made it to her hotel room door, she turned, smiled, and extended her hand. "Thanks for the lift," she said.

RJ took her hand, but instead of shaking it, he held it. "Your hand is so small in my hand," he said, looking down at how his big hand smothered hers. "You know what they say," he said, as he looked back up at her.

"About what?"

"About a brother with big hands."

Marti removed her hand from his grasp. "No, I haven't heard that one," she said, and they both laughed.

But she used her keycard to unlock her door. "Have a good one, Captain Jeffers."

"But aren't you going to invite me in?"

She shook her head. "No, I'm going to take myself a shower and call it a night. I'm drained."

She could see the disappointment in his eyes. He was pissed. "Can I at least use the restroom before I have to make that long drive back?" That was always one of his go-to lines that never missed.

Except this time. "There's a rest room downstairs," she said to him. "Have a nice rest of your evening," she added, went into the room, and closed *and locked* the door behind her.

RJ stood there momentarily fuming. "I know this bitch didn't just close that door in my face," he muttered to himself. But when she didn't open it back up claiming that she was joking, he realized his go-to line fell flat. And he left the corridor.

Still fuming when he got off the elevator and walked outside, he didn't expect to see Grant getting out of his car and heading toward the entrance. "What are you doing here?" he asked him.

Grant was inwardly fuming himself. "I thought I told you to stay away from her."

"I just gave her a ride back to her hotel room."

"And?"

"And nothing. A waste of my time. And yours too. That chick ain't opening that store for nobody. You can forget that," he added, as he headed back to his car.

Grant could feel his tense body sigh relief. The entire drive over was filled with rage that some player like RJ would coax her into sleeping with him the way every woman he'd ever asked slept with him, and he'd give her nothing in return but a broken heart. When even Grant could tell she'd had too many breaks already.

But Grant lingered until RJ drove off. He had to see for himself that Marti was okay, and that RJ really hadn't hurt her feelings or tried anything untoward with her.

But mainly he just wanted to see her again.

He entered the hotel's lobby.

CHAPTER SIXTEEN

Marti placed her hand under the shower water, felt that it was hot enough, and was about to remove her clothing when she heard knocks at her room door.

Room service already? she thought. She'd literally just ordered it! She was certain she could take a shower before they showed up. But they were there already?

She turned off the water tap and made her way out of the bathroom, past the king bed, the sofa, and the chair and dressing table, and made her way up to the door. But when she looked through the peephole and saw that it wasn't room service, but Chief McGraw, she hesitated. She was pleased to see him: she'd admit that. But she was worried too. Captain Jeffers failed, so he thought he'd give it a go? Were these men in Belgrave that hard up? It was becoming a definite turn off for her.

She opened the door with that same look he probably gave to her when she showed up, unannounced, at his home. "Hi."

But as soon as that door opened and Grant saw her face again, those warm feelings returned. Like clockwork. It was uncanny to him. "Are you okay?" he asked her.

Why wouldn't she be, she wanted to ask him. "I am, yes," she said instead.

He had his hands in his pants pockets. Although he was certain he had the look of a confident man since he didn't know any other way to look, inside he felt unsure of himself. Even foolish. Like why was he bothering this lady when she'd already given RJ the boot? Why did he have to see her?

He decided to just tell the truth. "You were gone when I finished up. I wanted to make sure you made it home safely."

Marti was touched by his concern. If that was what it was. "If you could call a hotel room home, then yes, I made it home just fine."

"Good. I know RJ can be a handful."

"Captain Jeffers?" She smiled. "Yes, he can."

"He's not used to women turning him down."

That seemed like a rather presumptuous thing to say to Marti. How would he know that he tried to hit on her and, more importantly, that she turned him down? "You must have seen him leaving. He just left a few minutes ago."

"Yeah, we met in the parking lot. But you said he just left. He had been in your room then, hun?"

Did she let him inside, was what he seemed to want to know, which kind of pleased her that he was displaying what could be construed as a bit of jealousy. She also noticed how the chief was taking glances of her rather than looking her dead on. As if there was more he wanted to say, but he couldn't figure out how to say it. "Everything okay, Chief?"

"Everything's good. I know it had to be tough for you to have to fire your weapon. Just wanted to make sure you were . . . handling it okay."

Now she was truly touched. "It was hard, I have to admit that. It's been a minute since I fired it. And I froze a little."

Grant looked at her with nothing but concern in his eyes. "You did?"

"Oh yeah. It's been four years since I've been in the line of duty you know? I definitely froze."

"What snapped you out of it?"

She decided to just tell the truth too. "You," she said.

Grant didn't understand. "Me?"

"I realized that if I didn't take him out, he was going to take you out. And that wasn't happening. Not on my watch. So I did what I

145

had to do."

Grant's heart soared. It wasn't just him! She was having those crazy feelings too. He smiled that smile that aged him, but that Marti was beginning to view as most attractive. "Glad I could be of help," he said, and they both laughed. "Although you disobeyed my direct order," he said to her playfully, pointing at her.

"Sorry, *not sorry,* about that." They laughed at that too.

And it all felt so organic and real again. They were back in their *no bullshit* zone. "Want to come in?" she asked him. He gladly said yes.

They walked over to the sofa. It wasn't a suite. Just a single room. But that was because the AG's office was paying for her room and board during her assignment, given her low salary, and they weren't trying to splurge. The king bed was in the one room, along with a desk and chair and the sofa, and the bathroom was just off from the main room.

She could remember going on vacations and staying in fancy hotels or extravagant Airbnb houses and condos, but that felt like so long ago and so far away that it no longer felt real. Because nowadays, if she had to pay for her own room and board, she would have been staying in a two-star motel if that. A Motel 6 at best. But a nice, three-star hotel like the one she was in? Nowadays it was an upgrade for her.

Grant removed his suit coat and flapped it over the back of the sofa before he sat down. Marti found herself staring at his body as she sat down. He was all muscle. Especially in his biceps. He was a big man.

"Did you find out anything new about why they targeted Karney's?" she asked Grant as he sat down.

"Nothing new. Appears to be some random act of violence by a couple of sick individuals. But once we get into both shooters' social media accounts, that should give us more insight."

But Marti still heard what he said earlier. "You believe it was a random shooting?"

Grant looked at her. "Yes." He studied her eyes. "But I take it you don't."

"Did you see the video?"

"I saw it, yes."

"Did you see the way the second gunman pretended to be a customer and ran in that office with the real customers and those employees when they were trying to get away from the gunfire?"

Grant nodded. "I saw it. So what?

147

What about it?"

"If you looked at his eyes, he seemed to be staring at one employee in particular."

Grant had not seen any such thing. "Was he?"

Marti nodded. "It was subtle, and you had to look really closely, but it's on that video. His eyes honed-in on that lady in the green pantsuit. And if you look even closer, you can see that she recognized him just before he started firing on her. It was only after he shot her repeatedly did he began shooting the others. As if to make it appear like a mass shooting."

Grant frowned. He watched that video twice and didn't see any of those nuances. "Why didn't you tell me this at the scene?"

"I tried to talk to you, but your men wouldn't let me anywhere near you. They said you were with the mayor or the chairman of the oversight board or the media. They gave me no access."

Grant exhaled. "That will change," he said to her.

"I sure hope so," she said to him.

He exhaled again. She could see that he was distressed. "You got me there," he said, "because I don't think I even looked at his eyes. I was totally focused on his gun."

"Like I said they weren't glaring examples. Very subtle. You had to look very closely."

"Don't make excuses for me," Grant said bluntly. "I dropped the ball. There's no two ways about it. I'll look into that. Thanks."

Marti loved once again how he wasn't a defensive man when given information he missed. Although it did worry her that he and his men seemed to miss a lot of basic, 101 policing techniques. "Perhaps you need to reconsider how your men are actually being trained."

When she said it, Grant suddenly got a bright idea. A way to keep her around him when her consultant gig was up. "Would you be interested in becoming that trainer?"

Marti was startled by such a question. "*Me*?" She stared at him. It was the first time he revealed to her, in words, that he just might be interested in her. His actions already suggested it, in a roundabout way, but she was never sure. Until now. He wanted her around him. He wanted to keep her around him. And that reality kind of alarmed her.

Mainly because she was not the kind of girl that went into anything halfway. Especially a relationship, if that was where he was trying to take it. She'd had too much pain. She knew

149

she couldn't bear any more. "I don't . . . I haven't . . . It never occurred to me to--"

"I understand." Grant knew he had exposed his budding feelings for her in that moment, and it was scaring the shit out of her. Was scaring him, too. "Just think about it. You don't have to give any answer tonight. Just mull over it for a few days."

She actually sighed relief. "I can certainly do that," she said. Then she smiled. "You know what I realized after Captain Jeffers asked to give me a lift?"

Grant looked at her. Why was she bringing RJ's name up? Did he manage to cast his spell on her too? "What did you realize?"

She grinned. "That I left my car at the station."

"Oh that!" He smiled. "I'll have one of my officers pick you up in the morning."

"Thanks so much. Because I sure didn't feel like going all the way to the station tonight to pick it up myself. Or deal with an Uber in the morning. Thanks."

"I should be thanking you."

"For what?"

"For saving my life." He wanted to add *in more ways than one*, but he didn't. Because she wouldn't believe it. But that was what it was beginning to feel like to him. She was rejuvenating him in ways he didn't think possible, and she didn't even know it.

"I'm just glad I didn't choke. Because I could have easily choked."

Grant studied her. "What happened to you, Markita?"

It was a tough question. Too tough. She had to maintain her barrier. "I'll make a deal with you, Chief. You don't tell me your sad stories, and I won't tell you mine."

But Grant was already shaking his head. "No deal." If their relationship was going to amount to anything, and that was a big *if*, it had to be real and honest and in the open.

But when he said no deal, Marti waited for him to smile or say he was just kidding. But he looked dead serious. Not as if he wanted to know her backstory just for curiosity sake, but as if he *needed* to know it.

It took several awkward seconds, but then it happened. For the first time in years, Marti said out loud what happened. "I gave my daughter a sweet sixteen birthday party. All of her friends were there and a few of my friends too. It was a lovely evening. But then one of the guys at the party, a crooked cop who shouldn't have been there, got into an argument over a card game and ended up shooting one of the players. And was about to start shooting some of the others. I yelled for him to drop his weapon, but he turned it on me instead."

Grant held his breath. Had she been shot? Was that her trauma?

"When he turned his gun on me, my training kicked in."

"Kill or be killed," said Grant.

Marti nodded. "Right. So that's what I did. I shot him repeatedly. They said I fired every bullet I had in my gun into him. But . . . But . . ."

He could see her soft eyes turn over into a look of terror that she was trying desperately to suppress. She folded her arms and her legs. She was struggling.

But he had to know. From her. Before he looked it up himself. "But what, Marti?"

"But one bullet, just one, went through Andy, that was his name, and it hit Jaleesa. It hit my little girl."

When she said those words, Grant's entire body slumped. "Oh God no," he said, his face a mask of concern.

He looked so anguished that it caused Marti to actually get distracted from her pain.

"Oh God no," he said again, and then he pulled her into his arms with a desperation to hold her that touched her soul. "I am so sorry, Marti. I am so sorry!"

He held her so sweetly that it caused tears to well up in her eyes. Those same tears she cried every single night. But always alone.

CHAPTER SEVENTEEN

For nearly ten straight minutes he just held her. The very idea of a mother realizing what she'd done to her child felt like a crushing blow to Grant. It was a miracle she was still standing. It was a miracle. He held her even tighter.

He was so concerned about her wellbeing that he didn't even notice that her nearness had caused him to have a hard on. It didn't even register to him.

It didn't register to Marti, either, as she began sobbing. He pulled her onto his lap and held her even tighter as she sobbed. Because she didn't hold back the way she did every night. The way she never let go. But in Grant's arms, she let go. She let it rip. As if she was finally unburdening herself. As if she was finally unleashing what had been choking her for four straight years.

Grant handed her his handkerchief as she sobbed. He held her tenderly as she was unable to stop herself from crying.

"How did you survive it?" he finally asked her. "How did you manage to live through something that horrific?"

"I don't know if I have lived through it," Marti responded. "I get by. I do what I need to do. But I don't know if you could call it living. It's been so hard," she said, and her sobbing increased. "When I tried to explain it to my friends, they understood it on some level, but they couldn't truly understand it. They needed me to get over it so they could move on too. But I couldn't get over it. So they moved on anyway."

"Fair weather friends," said Grant.

"They were good friends," said Marti. "But I made it too difficult. They couldn't handle it."

"Fuck them," said Grant as he held her tighter still. "It was your child. It was your tragedy, not theirs. And they couldn't be there for you? Fuck them," he said again.

Marti had never had anyone to fully understand how she felt. Because Grant was right. They all seemed to dismiss it for their own sakes and sanity. For their own selves.

She continued to cry. She continued to let it all out as if she was letting it out once and for all. She sobbed more than she ever had.

But when the sobbing finally stopped, she fully expected him to release her and get away from her. Why would he want to be around a disaster like her? Her friends had years invested in her, and they bounced. Why would he stick around?

But he continued to embrace her. It felt to Marti as if it wasn't even a question that he would stick around. And that warmed her hurting heart. They sat that way, in silence, for several more minutes.

Until Grant spoke up. "I used to be in the tech industry."

Marti went still. Captain Jeffers told her the chief never discussed his past. He never said why he sold his company and returned to his hometown. But he was telling her? It felt like a moment. A very important moment for him just as her revelation had been for her. She didn't say a word.

"I was flying high. Was about to take my company public. Wall Street was ready. I was ready. Things were truly looking up. I even had a woman in my life. Not a woman I loved, it was never that deep, but I at least liked her more than any of the others I'd been with."

That sounded strange to Marti. Was he saying he'd never been in love? A man his age? Did he even believe in love? Was she falling for that kind of guy? A guy guaranteed to break her heart? She listened closely. But she quickly realized it wasn't about that woman.

"I was on top of the world," Grant continued. "Then it all came crashing down."

There was a long pause. Marti wanted to look at him, to encourage him to continue, to say or do something in that silence. But she didn't. He had to tell it in his time, and in his way. She remained silent.

"I got word that Dana, my sister, was sick. Gravely so. And that she wasn't going to make it. She was my kid sister. She meant the world to me. Our parents were dead. She was all I had and I was all she had. She was my everything."

He paused again. "So I put the IPO on hold, flew to Montana where she lived, went to the hospital and stayed by her side. I never left her side. But she was gone just three weeks later."

Marti closed her eyes as tears stained her lids. Her ex-husband died young too, less than a year after they divorced. His killer? The big C: Cancer. Grant didn't say what his sister's poison was, and Marti wasn't ever going to ask.

"After Dana died," Grant continued with a hard exhale, "I tried to resume my life. I tried to move on. But I couldn't move at all. I started having panic attacks. Nightmares about disasters. I couldn't eat, I couldn't sleep,

I couldn't function. My very good tech company had a chance to become great, and I was ruining it for all those hardworking people that made it a success. So I decided to sell my interest in the company, which was sixty-four percent of the company, and I got out. I left California and moved back here, to Belgrave, to my hometown. I guess I kind of checked out too."

Marti waited for him to continue, but he said no more. That was when she spoke up. "How are you doing now?" she asked him.

He smiled a weak, insincere smile. "Not great. Still struggling."

"Why would you take a stressful job like police chief," Marti asked him, "if you knew you were still struggling?"

"For the distraction."

"Has it worked?"

Grant nodded. "Yes. It didn't make me a good policeman, but at least it gave me something to do every day."

"Are you saying you've never been a police officer before you became chief?"

"None of my predecessors were cops either. That's not how it works in Belgrave. Here, the police chief is appointed by the mayor and is more the administrator of the department. We do hands on, too, don't get me wrong, because whatever happens at the BPD the chief is ultimately the responsible party."

"You get all the blame."

Grant nodded. "We get all the blame. But no, none of the chiefs in Belgrave's history have ever been rank-and-file cops. And all of my predecessors, like myself, were appointed from the business sector."

"Perhaps that's the problem," said Marti.

Grant thought about it. "Perhaps so. But I agreed to accept the appointment because I knew I had to do something. It kept me going. Which was all I was asking for."

"That's a very low ask."

Grant knew it too, but that was why he said nothing more.

And they continued to sit in silence. It didn't take long, after that, for Grant to realize he had a hard on and for Marti to feel it beneath her. But they remained where they were. It was as if they both liked the feeling and didn't want it to end.

Until knocks were heard on the room door.

"That's room service," she said.

"I'll get it," he said, helped her off of his lap, and he went to the door to retrieve the wheeled cart filled with three covered trays.

"Lots of food for your little self," he said as he closed the door and wheeled it in.

She laughed. "I like to sample. I probably won't even touch ninety percent of it."

"I'll take the leftovers," Grant said as he pulled the cart over to the sofa. "I haven't eaten all day."

"You haven't?" Now she seemed concerned about him, which pleased him. "Why not? I at least took the time out to walk down the street and get me some lunch."

"That's the thing: I was pulled by every uppity muck in this town. I didn't have time to do anything but listen to their worries about what two mass shootings in one week would look like to the public."

"Then eat it all if you care to," she said as she stood up, although she was certain he was the kind of man that wouldn't do that to her. That he was going to leave her more than she could ever eat.

Why was she so certain about that, she couldn't say. But she was certain.

"While you eat, I'm going to go and take a shower. I never eat until I shower," she added.

Grant was already eating. "Sounds like a personal problem to me," he said, and they both laughed. And Marti went and took her shower. It felt as if they had unburdened their loads, and felt lighter.

Grant felt like a million bucks. He felt happy. And it wasn't just the food either, although it tasted fantastic to him. It was the easiness of their relationship, if he could even call it a relationship. But it all felt so natural to him.

But when he thought about the pain she had to have endured, his happiness was tempered with concern for her. Because he above all else cared about her. He didn't know why. He had only just met her. And it wasn't her story. He'd heard sad stories all his life from other females, horribly sad stories, but none of them moved him nearly as much as her story had.

But when he finished stuffing his face and still leaving her nearly half of everything (it was just that much food), he had to pee. She had to shower before she ate. He always had to pee after he ate. And it wasn't some *I can hold it until later* pee, either. He had to go and go now!

He eased the door open and peeped into the bathroom to make sure she was covered by the shower door or curtain. When he saw that a heavy white shower curtain covered the shower stall she was bathing in, he inwardly sighed relief and tiptoed to the toilet. He peed for a long time.

But when he finished, shook off the residual pee that always took its time to come out, then he forgot his incognito presence in that bathroom and flushed the toilet.

As soon as Marti heard a loud sound in the bathroom, she quickly flung open the shower curtain just as Grant was turning in her direction. He still had his penis out and his hand was still holding it.

Her eyes immediately moved down to that penis and she couldn't help but notice the thickness. His eyes were immediately drawn to her superfine brown bombshell of a body, and her nakedness he couldn't unsee. And they both were frozen in time, as if in suspended animation.

But Grant knew something that he could no longer suppress. He had to have her. He just had to.

Still staring at her, he kicked off his shoes, dropped his pants and briefs and stepped out of them, and began lifting his shirt over his head, revealing a hard, muscular chest, as he dropped the shirt and made his way to that shower stall.

Marti's heart was hammering when she saw the fullness of his nakedness, his hot body, and all she wanted was to be in his big arms again. Forget that it was too soon. Forget that he was technically her boss. She had to have him too.

And when he stepped inside of that shower, and placed his hands on the side of her face, and stared at her with a look of love so poignant that she wanted to cry, she knew he had her too. Right where he wanted her. Which was a position she promised herself to never allow herself to ever be in ever again. And she was about to back out. Until he began kissing her.

He kissed her so hard and with so much furious desperation that Marti surrendered her entire body to a man for the first time in years.

Grant could feel his fully-aroused, rock-hard penis pressed against her sumptuously soft body. And the desire to be inside of this particular woman became a need he could no longer forgo. An itch he had to scratch.

But he also could feel her hesitation when their naked bodies first met. He could feel her body begin to back away from his when he placed his hands on each side of her face. That was why he kissed her. He wanted her so badly that he needed her to want him too. And it happened! He could feel her hesitation dwindle as he kissed her with a ferocity he hadn't felt in decades. She was who he wanted. She was who he needed. She was the one.

And when she began to match the desire in his kiss, and her lips felt like water in a desert for him, it broke him. He hurried her backwards until her back slammed against the shower wall with his hand behind her to cushion her, and their kissing became even more epic.

He was a man who could no longer control his desire for her. He was a man who was not going to be denied. He wanted total control. And since she was a woman whose entire life was a neat little bow of control, and she wanted him to untie that bow, he took the reins. He was starved for her. And she wanted him to eat it up.

She didn't think he could kiss her any more passionately than he already had, but he did. He went to town on her mouth. His control became out of control. And it felt like freedom to both of them. Finally their past was no longer dictating their future, and the here and now was unleashed. They were in the moment. And they stayed there.

CHAPTER EIGHTEEN

When he began to move down, to her breasts and between her legs, she let out so loud a moan that it echoed throughout the shower. Even the running water could not contain it.

Then he placed his hands beneath her small thighs and lifted her up. And that was when the rubber hit the road. It was getting too real for cautious Marti, and he could feel her hesitation again.

That was when he leaned his mouth to her ear. "It's been over eight years since I've had unprotected sex."

Marti looked into his eyes.

"Eight years, baby," he said to her. "Eight long years. Please believe me."

She believed him. And it wasn't because she was caught up in the moment either. She flat believed him.

And when her eyes gave her consent, he believed her and entered her.

It was meant to be slow and easy, but as soon as he *touched her* so intimately, his patience failed him, and he thrust it in!

Marti's moans increased exponentially

when he entered her so dramatically, but foreplay had been the key that allowed her to enjoy every inch of his thickness.

They were so enthralled with the feelings that it didn't take long before they were cumming. It couldn't take long. They were too starved for each other.

But after they came, and as Grant was leaned against Marti and they were both unable to control their breathing, they both knew it wasn't over yet. It was just the beginning.

After getting out of the shower and drying off, Grant lifted Marti up, kissing her again, and they went to bed. But once he got her under covers, he brought the tray of food he had left for her to eat, and she ate it up, with him helping her.

Once they were both full again, and he had removed the tray, they laid side by side, staring at each other. But when he kissed her, it was as if they were back in the shower. Those feelings erupted once more, and they were at it again.

When Grant woke up the next morning, it was six-eighteen am. He looked over at Marti, who was still in his arms, and he smiled. She slept so peacefully. She got a raw deal in life, but she didn't give up. She still showed up. It warmed his heart.

For nearly ten minutes he laid there staring at Marti. Sweet. That was the word that came to his mind as he watched her. She was so sweet. He could see himself spending the rest of his life with a woman like her. He could see himself falling madly in love with her. She could work wonders for his sour disposition.

But could he work wonders for her? A grumpy old player like him? And what if she wasn't who she presented herself to be? What if she was after his money just like all the others were, but knew how to camouflage it better? What if she broke his heart just as definitively as his beloved sister had?

Dana had already broken it in two.

Marti would break it to pieces.

People survived a broken heart. Nobody could survive a crumbled one.

Which brought him back to earth. What was he doing all out in space talking of falling in love anyway? That wasn't his lane. He didn't know shit about falling in love.

But something was happening. He knew that. Something that pricked at him in ways nothing else ever had. Could it be he was falling in love? Or was it all just lust?

Because that was strong too. So strong that he was getting a hard on watching her. But he knew that came later. That didn't explain that hard-hitting feeling of familiarity he felt when he first laid eyes on her. And how she warmed his heart even then. Something was happening. Could it be love? To him, what else could it be?

But he knew he was out of his depth. He'd never been in love a day in his long life. He honestly wouldn't know that kind of love if it slapped him in the face. It would be just that new to him. And he wasn't the kind of man to try new things.

He slowly slid his penis out of her vagina as he realized his awakening had awakened his penis and it was coming back to life once again. He threw the covers off of his naked body, made sure her naked body remained covered, and eased out of bed. His quick morning meetings with his frontline officers were always at eight am, and he was never late. He needed to go home to change clothes. But since he'd already established that she didn't have to be in until ten, he decided against waking her. He wanted her to continue her peaceful, sweet sleep.

He dressed, left her a note, stared at her a few seconds longer, and then he left her hotel room.

But it wasn't until much later, when he was walking into the police station, did he realize an amazing fact. He suddenly realized that he had managed to sleep all night long for the first time in nearly a decade. No nightmares. No waking up in a cold sweat. No sitting outside just to keep his sanity intact. He slept like a baby. With Markita in his arms.

He smiled as he entered the station. He felt as if he was walking on air.

CHAPTER NINETEEN

Later that morning Grant stood in Lieutenant Pete Kerrigan's office with a cup of hot coffee in his hand. Pete sat behind his desk trying to convince his boss that there had to be a connection.

"Think about it, sir. We've only had one mass shooting in Belgrave in its seventy-seven-year history. Just one. Yet in a matter of days we've have two back-to-back? Come on now, Chief. Some things make sense and some things don't. There has to be a connection."

"A connection to what?"

They all looked when they heard that voice. It was RJ walking into Pete's office.

"Those two mass shootings have to be connected," Pete said.

"They have to be," RJ agreed.

"But chief don't think so."

RJ looked at Grant. But when he did, he smiled. "Look at you."

Grant frowned. "What are you looking at me for?"

"You shaved."

When RJ said it was when Pete noticed

it too. "That's true."

"Your suit isn't wrinkled. Your eyes aren't bloodshot."

"I didn't know you had blue eyes, chief," Pete joked. "I thought their natural color was red."

He and RJ laughed.

"Very funny," said Grant, although he said it in a way that allowed his men to feel at ease teasing him. He was in a good mood.

"What gives?" RJ asked. Then he remembered last night and how Grant didn't immediately head back to his car when RJ told him Nash wasn't putting out. "You got some, didn't you?"

Grant's demeanor immediately changed. He wasn't about to let his captain disrespect Marti. "Knock that shit off, RJ." He even pointed at him. "Now I mean it. And that goes for you, too, Pete. She's here to do a job and you guys will stop trying to get in her panties and start accommodating her."

"Okay." RJ knew he was on the right track, but he also knew Grant could be a bear if you got on his wrong side. "I apologize."

"You apologizing?" asked Pete. "Believe that if you want, Chief."

"I'm not saying there isn't a connection," Grant said, but Pete interrupted him.

"Speaking of the devil," Pete said, and Grant and RJ looked out of his window that faced the front parking lot. Marti was getting out of a patrol car.

Grant's heart squeezed with affection as soon as he saw her. Although she was dressed in her usual elegance, this time in a red herringbone jacket, a light-blue sheer shirt and red slacks, he remembered vividly how she looked in that shower with no clothes on at all. And how desperately he wanted her then. And still wanted her now.

"Wonder what it's like to have a piece of that?" Pete asked as they all looked at her with lust in their eyes.

"Didn't Grant just tell you to cut that shit out?" RJ said.

Pete grinned. "You tapped that last night when you took her to her hotel. Didn't you?"

Grant looked at Pete.

And Pete quickly realized the chief wasn't going to play that game. "I was joking around, chief, honest. I'll cut it out." Then Pete and RJ glanced at each other as if their boss was taking it way too serious for it to be nothing.

They continued to watch Marti as she walked over to her car that had been left at the station overnight and grabbed some papers off of the front seat to stuff into her briefcase.

"You think she's sending bad reports to the AG about us?" Pete asked the chief.

"Don't do anything bad and she won't have any bad reports to send," Grant responded.

"But what if she make stuff up. What if she's a liar?" asked Pete.

"She's no liar," Grant said with such confidence that his two senior staff members glanced at each other again.

Outside, after Marti had finished stuffing more paperwork into her briefcase and locked her car again, she began heading for the entrance. She'd already felt a sense of excitement when she saw the chief's Mercedes parked in his designated parking space, because it meant he was in the office and she would hopefully get to see him again.

Not that she thought it was wise to be so giddy about some man when she was only in town to do a very specific job, but she couldn't help it. After last night, he won her over. She was already warming to him simply because he treated her so well, but the way he treated her last night took that warm to hot. She had the hots for him. He did things to her body that no man had ever done. Not even her husband during their best days.

He left her a note to let her know he had gone home to change. He told her that one of his officers would be there at nine-forty-five to pick her up, and that he wanted her to eat breakfast before his man arrived. When he wrote that he liked his women with meat on their bones, she smiled. When he then wrote that she'd better behave, she laughed. They had that kind of relationship. Very sincere and even playful. Which wasn't either one of their personalities. That was what made it special to her. Then he wrote that she could call him Grant, and he signed his note with the letter G. Just G. Which felt special to her too.

But it wasn't until she was walking into the station did she realize that something remarkable had happened to her last night. She realized that she didn't cry herself to sleep for the first time in four years. That loneliness and *longingness* didn't overtake her when the darkness came. Because she was in Grant's arms. And his arms felt like a cocoon. She felt safe and secure there. It felt like home.

She heard conversations coming from Lieutenant Kerrigan's office and when she looked in that direction and saw Captain Jeffers and the chief, she headed for that office. A part of her was hesitant. She knew their relationship, such as it was, had to remain under wraps around his men. But she was never a faker. Could she truly hide that excitement she felt just knowing she would be around Grant again? She even remembered how scared she was when she first woke up and realized he wasn't there. She thought he might have viewed what they did last night as a big mistake, and he wanted out already. Until she saw his note.

"Good morning," she said to the men when she walked over to the office door.

Although nobody said good morning to her, not even the chief, she noticed RJ had glanced at his Rolex. Which begged the question for Marti. She was so concerned about Grant's lifestyle that she never even considered RJ's. Had he come to the force as a rich man too? And if he had, what kind of force was this?

"Wish I had your hours," RJ said as he glanced at his watch.

"Or are you on CP time?" Pete asked with a grin. "RJ told us about that."

"Her hours are 10 to 5," Grant stepped in and said, saving her from having to do so. But she felt he still could have at least said good morning back to her.

"Did you have a good night's sleep?" RJ

asked her, and Pete attempted to suppress his grin.

"Yes. Did you?" Marti responded, knowing why RJ would ask that. He was assuming something happened between her and the chief. Unless, she thought with some degree of horror, the chief told him what happened between them!

"I slept well," RJ said. "Very well. Thank you for asking." That did it. Pete burst into laughter.

They were really very juvenile to Marti.

"Come on in," Grant said to her and that, at least, made her feel better.

But it was kind of jarring for Marti to be in the same room with the man that had been inside of her, not once, but twice last night. She still felt those feelings. She still felt that emptiness when she woke up and realized he was no longer inside of her.

For Grant, he wanted in again as soon as she entered the office and stood across the room from him. He knew why she made certain not to get next to him. She wanted to keep it professional while they were on the clock. He understood that. But just seeing her again brought back last night in vivid detail. In that shower. And later in bed. How they ate together and cried together and laughed together. It was one of the most revealing nights he'd ever had.

"We have a debate going on," he said to her when he could tell she was uneasy. "My men seem to believe the two mass casualty events were connected. I say the jury is still out. What say you?"

But before Marti could say a word, Sergeant Carter came into the office looking flustered. "We got him, chief."

"Who?"

"The Wafer House shooter."

As soon as Carter said those words, everybody stood up and began hurrying toward the office exit. "Where?" Grant asked.

"The Lamplight Trailer Park over on Dakota Street. He's all the way in the back. He refuses to come out."

"Who's there now?"

"A few patrol cars. SWAT is on its way."

"Have the beats evacuate that trailer park," Grant ordered as they hurried for the lobby, "and tell them to cordon off that entire street north and south."

"Yes sir. But get this, Chief," Carter said and all of them looked at him.

"What?"

"He says he'll only come out if you let him talk to her."

Everybody stopped. Grant frowned. He was certain he didn't hear that right. "Talk to who?"

"To her. Lieutenant Nash."

It was Marti's time to frown. "Why would he want to talk to me?"

"He didn't say."

Everybody looked at Marti. "You know him?" Pete asked her.

"Of course I don't know him! If I knew him I would have said so already."

"Then why he wanna talk to you?"

"How should I know?"

But all Grant saw was danger for Marti. "You're staying here," he said to her.

"What if I can help get him out of that trailer?"

"She's got a point, Chief," said RJ. "He's a danger to this community. They want him caught, not holed up in some trailer."

"And if she can help," Pete said, "we need that help."

But Grant was never that easily persuaded. "She's not going," he said again and began heading for the exit. His men followed him.

Marti did too. "I have a job to do, Chief," she said, causing him to stop and look at her.

Was she going to defy him? "I said you

are not going."

"It's my job to be in the field. Not hanging around an office. It's my job, Chief. I've got to do my job."

Her sincerity was only matched by his concern for her safety. Why would some crazed gunman want to speak to her? But he'd already warned his men to not interfere with her authority. He knew he couldn't either. He continued heading for the exit.

RJ and Pete hopped in Pete's car, while Grant, they noticed, opened the passenger door of his car for Marti and then he got in behind the steering wheel. His two men sped off ahead of him, but he was right behind them.

And he was pissed. "If I tell you that you aren't doing something, don't you dare defy me in front of my men!" he yelled at Marti.

"I have to do my job even if it means defying you."

Grant sped through a red light and continued speeding through the streets of Belgrave. Then he looked at her again. "I told you to remain outside and you went into Karney's anyway. That worked out, yes it did, but it could have gone horribly wrong. This is not going horribly wrong. I don't care what that lunatic wants," he warned her, "and I don't care if it is your job, you aren't going into that trailer.

And that's not debatable! Do I make myself clear, Markita? You aren't going in that trailer."

Marti wanted to remind him that she was supposed to make her own decisions when it came to her observations, even though he was technically her boss while she was in his jurisdiction. But she still had autonomy. The AG's office made that clear.

But she held her tongue. It was a card she was willing to play if she had to. But for the sake of their brand-new *situationship*, which suddenly felt frosty again, she hoped it was a card she didn't have to play.

CHAPTER TWENTY

The entire street was cordoned off and the residents of the trailer park were being evacuated to a church a block over.

A patrolman lifted the yellow tape and Grant and Marti walked through. The police cars were across the street from the trailer in question, forming a barricade for protection. Everybody on scene, including RJ and Pete, were behind those cars.

The detective in charge of the case, with a blowhorn in hand, hurried over to the chief.

"We've got a line of communication?" Grant asked him.

"Yes sir. But his request hasn't changed. He'll only speak to the consultant."

"Does he know me by name?" Marti asked the detective.

"It doesn't appear so, no ma'am. He keeps saying *that consultant*."

"Has he said why he wants to talk to me?"

That was a negative for the detective too. "He's not telling us anything. He'll only talk to you."

"He apparently has something major to

tell her, Chief," said Pete.

"Probably about the shooting at Karney's," said RJ, "since both of those suspects are dead and the community is convinced both mass shootings are related."

"He wants to talk to her, Chief," the detective said again. "And only her."

"Did he specify where?" asked Grant.

The detective nodded his head. "Yes sir. He wants her inside with him."

Grant stood there as his men continued to speak as if it was even a possibility. But Grant knew better. He knew they were out of their minds if they thought he was going to let Marti go anywhere near that murderer.

When they kept on talking about it as if it was only a question of logistics, Grant decided to put a period to it. "That's not happening," he said bluntly. "Are there any hostages inside that trailer?" he asked the detective, moving on. "Or do we even know?"

"We asked and he said nobody's in there. His neighbors said he lives alone."

"Well at least that," said RJ.

"Have you sent in a backdoor team yet?" Marti asked the detective.

Everybody looked at her. "What's that?" Grant asked her.

The lack of knowledge of basic police

work in this department astounded Marti still. Was every high ranking official on the force rich fat cats with no real police experience too? "While we distract the shooter up front with conversation or whatever we need to do to keep his attention, you need to get SWAT or another team of cops to go into that trailer through the backdoor."

"Why would we risk our men when we can burn that bastard down to the ground?" asked RJ. "All the people he's already killed."

"But what if he has intel on the shooting at that grocery store? At Karney's?" Marti said. "If we can take him alive, we need to do that."

"But I thought you agreed the two shootings weren't related," Grant said.

"I didn't say they weren't related. I said the motives might be different. But they could be a part of a network. The time of both incidences are just too close to rule that completely out."

Grant exhaled. That made sense too! "Get SWAT over here," Grant said as he went to the trunk of his car. When Marti saw him pull out a bulletproof vest, her heart dropped. She hurried over to him.

"You aren't going in," she said as if she was the boss.

"Check her out," said RJ with a grin.

"You're ordering the chief around now?" asked Pete.

"I mean why are you going in, Chief? That's a job for SWAT."

"I don't want anybody going rogue in that trailer and decide to shoot when shooting isn't necessary. I'll be leading the charge," he said as he put on his vest.

"But you should let the police handle that," she insisted.

Everybody looked at her. Including Grant, who continued to put on his vest. "What are you stupid?" asked Pete. "He's the chief of police!"

He's a businessman with zero experience as a cop when he became chief of police, Marti wanted to remind them. But she held her tongue. She was too worried about Grant. She wished she had let RJ's suggestion stand. "Maybe we could just burn it down like Captain Jeffers said," she said to Grant, and Pete quickly elbowed RJ.

Grant knew why she said it. She was worried about him. But she was right: They needed to take that shooter in alive just in case there was a network of mass shooters spacing out their crimes. He ignored her suggestion. "RJ, I'll radio in when we're in position," he said as he opened his front driver seat door. "I want you to then start a conversation with the shooter. Let him know the consultant has arrived and she'll be coming in. But ask him questions about how can he guarantee her safety and shit like that. Don't make it too easy on him or he'll know we're bullshitting him. We'll get in and try to keep his ass alive. But you've got to keep him distracted."

"Will do, Chief," RJ said as Grant and the three-man SWAT team hopped into his Mercedes.

But Grant took another look at a very-distressed Marti and pressed down his window. "Don't you move from that spot," he ordered her. "You hear me?"

She was reluctant, but she nodded her head. For a quick second, they exchanged a look that made clear he knew she was worried about him because he was worried about her. And then he drove away.

"Did you see that?" Pete whispered to RJ.

"Why are they going in the Chief's car?" Marti asked them. "SWAT doesn't have an armored vehicle?"

RJ laughed. "Gal where you think you at?" Pete asked her. "This ain't no Memphis! Memphis has over six hundred thousand citizens to support them. We barely got fifty thousand. Who's gonna pay for all this armored stuff you're talking about?"

But Marti was unable to shake her anguish, and she knew Pete and RJ saw it. That was why hooking up with Grant was a horrible idea. She was worried sick about him. To her, he was the sweetest, kindest man she'd ever known. To her, he was no cop, but was an administrator who had no business leading any charge to detain a murderer. "What are you going to say to distract him?" she asked RJ.

"What the chief told me to say."

"But I mean what are you going to actually say?"

"None of your damn business," RJ said, tiring of her heavy-handedness. "I'm a captain. You are, *or were*, a lieutenant. I outrank your ass any day of the week. Stay in your lane."

But even that unnecessarily hostile conversation didn't rile Marti. Her entire focus was on Grant.

And when Grant radioed in that he and SWAT were in position, she watched RJ with an eagle's eye take the reins.

RJ began speaking in the bullhorn. "Hello, Shooter?" Then he looked at the detective. "What's his name again?"

Marti couldn't believe it. She snatched the bullhorn away from RJ. "This is Marti Nash," she said as RJ attempted to grab it back. "This is the consultant you said you would like to speak with?"

"Not out there," the shooter yelled back. "You got to come in here!"

"Why inside? Why can't we talk like we're talking now?"

"Because I don't want them to hear what I got to say."

"Who's them?" Marti asked him.

"Them cops!" Emotion was in his voice. "They're trying to destroy me."

RJ rolled his eyes. "Nobody's trying to destroy that nut-brain."

But all Marti wanted was to keep the shooter engaged in conversation with her. "Why would you say they're trying to destroy you?"

"Because they are!"

"Can you name who you're talking about?"

"Why are you believing that bullshit?" Pete asked her.

"Give me a name," Marti said into the bullhorn. She was singularly focused.

"They know who they are. I didn't shoot nobody!"

That comment surprised Marti. "They have you on tape."

"That ain't me and they know it! I would never kill anybody. What I look like killing and maiming all those people?"

But then Grant's voice could be heard over the radio yelling "*Police! Drop your weapon!*"

Marti held onto the bullhorn with both hands as she listened to the interchange. She prayed there would be no gunfire, and there wasn't. Just a lot of movement as if they were tackling their suspect or something equally physical. "*Cuff him and frisk him,*" she then heard the chief say. And then he said into the radio: "*We got him,*" and all the cops out there erupted in applause. Marti nearly dropped the bullhorn she was so relieved.

But then RJ snatched it from her. "Pull that stunt again and I'll make it my business to kick your ass out of Dodge. You feel me?"

Marti and RJ looked into each other's eyes. The only blacks at the scene, there should have been some sense of tribalism, but there wasn't. No two people, Marti felt, could have been more dissimilar.

But when Grant came out of the front door with the shooter in handcuffs, she hurried toward him. RJ and Pete hurried too.

But the shooter was looking at Marti. "You that consultant?"

"Yes."

"They gonna get you too," he said as Grant turned him over to two patrolmen and they began walking him to a patrol car.

"Who's they?" Marti asked him. "And why would they want to get me?"

"Because you ain't crooked like them. They're all crooks, every one of them. I didn't kill nobody. And look what they doing to me."

"Get him out of here!" Grant ordered as the patrolmen hurried their suspect to the patrol car.

While RJ and Pete talked with the SWAT team, Marti moved over to Grant, who was taking off his bulletproof vest. "You're okay?"

"Yup."

"He didn't resist?"

"That's the crazy part," said Grant. "He didn't even have a gun."

Marti was astonished to hear that. "He didn't?"

"Not even a knife. No weapons whatsoever."

"That's unusual right? Even for a town like this?"

"Hell yeah it's unusual. I couldn't

believe it either until we cuffed him and," Grant started saying when they all suddenly heard a single gunshot. It came from the patrol car.

They all ran over to the car, led by Grant, but Marti was right on his tail.

When they got over there, the patrolman who had taken custody of the suspect had his weapon drawn, and the suspect, a close-range gunshot wound to the head, was slumped in his seat obviously dead. But she checked his vitals anyway.

"What the hell happened?" Grant asked the patrolman.

"He kept spitting on me, Chief, in my face and everywhere, so I pulled my gun on him and warned him to cut that shit out. Then he head-putted me, causing me to fall against him, and my gun went off."

"He was in handcuffs!" Marti yelled out at the officer. "Why didn't you just move your face out of his range, and then put a spit guard on him?"

"I didn't mean to shoot him!" the officer yelled back. "My gun went off. It was an accident!"

"Who are you, Barney Fyfe?" a still-angry Marti asked him. "How could your gun just go off that easily? You're a police officer!"

But the cop was sticking to his story,

even though it was a very unlikely story to Marti. She looked at the other cops. They were nodding as if it was a reasonable tale to them. She looked at Grant. Was he buying that bullshit too?

Grant looked flustered to her, but she couldn't tell if he was flustered because their suspect was dead and some serious questions would, or at least *should* arise, or was he flustered because his officer was in trouble? When the chief snatched his officer's gun before he *accidentally* shot somebody else, Marti decided he was going to protect his cop.

"Get out of here," Grant ordered him. Then he ordered one of the detectives to go with him and take a statement.

"I didn't mean to shoot him, Chief," the officer said again as he and the detective were leaving the scene. Another bad idea to Marti.

But it all seemed too pat for Marti. Just after the shooter said they had the wrong guy and that they were out to destroy him, he ended up dead in police custody?

Grant might have been buying it, but Marti wasn't.

But it wasn't like he gave her a chance to investigate further. They all seemed to be circling their wagons. They all seemed more concerned about how it looked rather than why it happened.

"Have we heard from City Hall?" RJ asked the senior officers that surrounded them.

"They called to let us know the mayor's on his way."

"Damn," said RJ. "He's on his way to take a victory lap because we caught the shooter and caught him alive. Now he's dead. Damn."

"He's gonna have your hide, Chief," said Pete. "The citizens of Belgrave are convinced the two mass shootings were connected to each other, and they wanted answers from the lone surviving shooter. Now this. He may fire you for real this time."

Grant wasn't thinking about the mayor or his future as the chief of police. The BOBs didn't let Dooney hire who he wanted as chief, and the BOBs weren't going to let him fire him to put in place who he wanted as chief. Grant was worried about Marti.

"How are we gonna handle this, Chief?" the detective in charge of the investigation asked him.

But Grant frowned, showing his frustration. "How the hell should I know? This shit just happened! You make sure you secure this scene and inside that trailer too. Make sure everybody's doing their job. The mayor's coming with cameras. This is supposed to be a triumph for him. Those cameras better not show anything we're doing wrong onsite that those ambulance-chasing *got*damn lawyers can later use against us in the lawsuit that's sure to come."

"Yes sir," the detective said, and all of the senior staff walked away to avoid the chief's ire too.

The chief finally looked at Marti.

"That's a bullshit story," Marti said. "You know that, right?"

The chief didn't respond.

"He said the suspect spat all over him, including in his face. I didn't see any spit on that officer whatsoever. Then he said the suspect head-butted him so hard that he fell against him. But there's no evidence of a head-butt either. It's bullshit, Grant. It's all bullshit."

"And what do you suggest I do about it?" Grant had an edge to his voice. He felt as if he was being pulled from both sides.

But Marti had no such feelings. "You should fire him," she said forcefully too. "That's what you should do about it."

"Fire him? That's your suggestion? I fire him so I can just tee up every damn lawyer in this town looking to defend the perp's family and force the city to pay out more money than it can afford? That's your suggestion?"

"Bump the money!" Marti yelled. "It's called doing the right thing. That man was in handcuffs. That man said he wasn't the shooter."

"Well guess what? The video says differently!"

"Are we sure about that? Are you certain about that? That video could have been altered."

Grant frowned. "*Altered*?"

"With A.I., yes. It's possible, Grant."

"So is life on Mars. But are we living there now?" Then he settled back down. "I want you to get an officer to take you back to your car. I want you to get in it and go back to your hotel. It's going to be a long day. I don't want any of this shit blowing back on you."

Marti frowned. "Why would it blow on me?"

"Because they need as many scapegoats as they can get. I'm the head of the police force. I'm always their target. But you're the new face in town. The mayor and his office are going to do everything in their power to discredit the governor through you."

"I don't even know the governor. I've never even seen him in person before in my life."

"You know that and I know that. They know it too. But does this bloodthirsty town knows it?"

"And how can the mayor blame you? What that officer did wasn't your fault. He can't blame you."

"He can and he will. I have to stay in the fire. But you don't. You're getting out of here. I'll get somebody to drive you back to the station."

But Marti wanted intel. An insider that might know more than the chief was willing to tell her. "I can ask if Captain Jeffers can drive me back," she said.

Grant looked at her. "Didn't he try to come onto you the last time he drove you anywhere?"

How would he know that? "It was no big deal."

But Grant looked as if it was a major deal. "You stay away from him. You hear me?"

"He only asked to use my bathroom."

"Do you hear me, Markita?"

The chief seemed so concerned that she couldn't help but hear him. "Yes sir."

Then he exhaled. Looked around and saw an unattractive chubby cop chewing the fat with some of the other cops. "Cranston!" he called out.

Cranston looked nervous when he heard the chief call his name. "Sir?"

Grant motioned for him to come over. Then Grant looked at Marti. He wanted to pull her into his arms. But he knew what gossip that would spurn. He managed to sneak in a hard squeeze of her arm instead. "I'll come over there as soon as I can get away."

"Okay," Marti said. She wanted that hug as badly as he wanted to give it to her.

Grant ordered Officer Cranston to take her to the station so she could pick up her car. As they were walking away, she glanced back at Grant. She was worried about him and it showed on her face.

So much so that RJ and Pete, who had been watching her and Grant's encounter, saw it too. "Who do they think they're fooling?" Pete asked. "The chief's tapping the shit out of that ass just as sure as I'm standing here."

"Forget them," RJ said. "You get to that patrolman that shot the perp. Tell him good job. But make sure he'd better keep his mouth shut."

Pete looked at RJ. "That was a close call."

"Too close," said RJ. "That's a problem."

"We eliminated the problem though."

"But what if it hadn't been one of our guys taking him to the station? What if he wasn't as quick on his feet and didn't pull that trigger? We're getting sloppy. They aren't gonna like that. We've got to tighten this ship before it takes us all down."

RJ looked at Pete, as if to remind him of just how serious their situation truly was, and then he walked away.

CHAPTER TWENTY-ONE

Marti had showered, put on her bathrobe, and had been watching news accounts all evening by the time knocks were heard on her hotel room door. She had to suppress the urge to run to the door, fling it open, and fall into Grant's arms. That was how much she missed him.

But she pulled herself together and took her pretty time going to that door. But when she opened it and saw that it was indeed the chief, and when he walked in and pulled her into his arms even as he was still closing the door, her heart melted. She couldn't hold back. She began embracing him as vigorously as he was embracing her. And when he began kissing her, and she matched his need, it became a long, hot, passionate kiss. She could feel him getting harder and harder against her thigh.

But she pulled back. He continued to hold her as she looked into his tired eyes. "I saw you on TV at that long-behind press conference."

"It's the story of the year around Belgrave," Grant said as he kept pressing his rock-hard penis against her, and as he continued to keep his arms around her slender, elegant body.

"You looked exhausted," Marti continued.

"I was exhausted."

"You look even more so now." Then she patted his barreled chest as she pulled away from him. "Go take a shower, you'll feel better. I'll order room service for us."

"For us? You haven't eaten yet?"

"I was waiting on you."

Grant wasn't accustomed to anybody considering his needs. "It's ten at night. Why would you wait so long?"

"I didn't want you to have to eat alone."

Grant smiled. That simple gesture warmed his heart. And he pulled her into his arms again and kissed her again.

Then he pulled back, his hands squeezing her butt, as he looked at her. "I used to prefer eating alone." Then he kissed her nose. "Not anymore," he said, squeezed her butt even harder, and then released her.

She smiled. "That squeeze hurt," she said, rubbing her butt.

"Serves you right," he said with a smile, as he made his way to the bathroom. "Not eating all day to wait on my sorry ass. Serves you right," he added playfully, as he closed the bathroom door behind him.

Marti smiled and ordered room service. If only Jaleesa was here, she thought. She used to worry about Marti's poor choice in men all the time. But Marti was certain J would have loved Grant. Just loved him. And Grant, if she was reading him right, would have loved her daughter too. Tears began to well up in her eyes, but she quickly wiped them away.

CHAPTER TWENTY-TWO

They ate heartily, in bathrobes in bed, as they watched the eleven o'clock news replay a significant portion of that press conference. Grant could see what Marti meant.

"Damn. I look like I could barely sit up there," he said.

"They kept asking the same questions over and over. I would have been exhausted too." Then she looked at him. "What's to become of the cop that shot the suspect? You nor the mayor really answered that question. All you guys would say is that you can't discuss active investigations."

"Because we can't. He's on desk duty for now, pending an investigation."

"But that entire press conference was about an active investigation: those two mass shootings. That's my point."

Grant nodded his head. "And your point is well taken. But that's politics. The mass shootings are a problem, and they want the public to know everything."

"You view yourself as a politician?" she asked him as his phone rang.

"No way. I hate politics," he said as he motioned for her to hand him his phone since he inadvertently placed it on the night stand that was next to her side of the bed. "But that's the game I have to play."

But as Marti was handing Grant his phone, she could see the name Ingrid on the Caller ID. She handed it to him and watched closely as he looked at the Caller ID and then swiped it so that it would shut off. Then he sat it on his nightstand.

But as they continued to eat, that phone call was weighing heavily on Marti. And she decided now was as good a time as any to bring it up. "Who was that?" she asked him.

"Pardon?"

"That phone call. Who was that?"

"Somebody I know."

"Named Ingrid?"

"Yes."

"Somebody you've dated before?"

He glanced at her as he chewed his steak. Was she one of those insecure, jealous kind of females? He didn't see her as that type, but he could be wrong. "Yes," he said.

Marti knew it made her seem petty, but she needed to know what she was getting herself into. "What is she to you?" she asked as casually as she could. "Your girlfriend?"

Grant looked at her. "Would you have slept with me, and be sitting in this bed with me, had you known I had a girlfriend?"

"Of course not."

"I don't have a girlfriend," he said to her. *Other than the one sitting beside me right now*, he wanted to add, but decided it was too soon.

Marti would have liked for him to add that disclaimer, but she knew it was early days too.

"She's a friend of mine," Grant said to put a period on it.

But that only led to another question. "A friend with benefits?"

He hesitated. "Yes."

He could see a look of concern wash over Marti's face. And he sought to clarify. "I haven't been celibate, Markita," he said to her. "Not in the least. But what I whispered to you in that shower last night is still true. I haven't had unprotected sex in years. Many years. Except with you."

But he could tell she needed more from him. Something he'd never been willing to give to any woman ever. Except now. "And I have no intentions of sleeping with anybody else but you," he added.

It was a monumental admission from a man like him, and he could tell she appreciated that it was.

She leaned over and kissed him. Then she smiled. "You taste like steak."

"When we finish eating," he said playfully, "I'm going to find out what you taste like. And it better not be steak."

She laughed. And they finished eating.

Grant got out of bed and placed their trays on the room service cart. Then he rolled it out into the hall. When he came back in and closed the door behind him, he went to the bathroom to pee one of his *after eating* longwinded pees.

Marti removed her robe, revealing her naked body, and got under the covers. But when his phone rang again while he was peeing and she was able to lift up slightly to see the Caller ID from his nightstand, she saw the name of another woman. This one named Allison. Which gave her pause. She almost put back on her robe and got out of bed. Was he a cheater like all those other men she'd been with? Was she about to make yet another mistake in a lifetime of mistakes with men? She always fell for the wrong one.

But Grant came back into the bedroom almost as soon as she had contemplated ending whatever this was. He looked at the Caller ID of his still-ringing phone, ended the call without answering the phone, but this time he turned his phone face down on his nightstand. Marti noticed that too. But then he removed his robe, revealing his nakedness, and got in bed beside her.

They laid on their sides face to face.

Marti placed her hand on the side of his most attractive face. It wasn't lost on her that he had shaved that morning after they first slept together, and that his suit wasn't wrinkled the way it usually was, and his eyes were clear as crystal, not their usual redness, although they looked tired and drained in that moment. But she could see that he was taking better care of himself already, which pleased her. "Did the mayor threaten to fire you again?"

"On camera, no. Off camera, about ten times."

"But the BOBs won't let him."

Grant was surprised to hear her say that. "What do you know about the BOBs?"

"I know they're the *Belgrave Oversight Board*. I know they're the power brokers in this town and they want to keep you in power. But *why* is my question?"

"Because they're rich." Then he looked at her. "And so am I. I'm one of them."

"Why did you look at me like that when you said that?"

"Like what?"

"Like the way you looked at me when you said you were rich."

"I wanted to see your reaction. Money is what most of the women I've been with, no, not most, but *all* of the women I've been with, wanted from me."

"I'm not after your money."

Grant continued staring at her.

Marti smiled. "You actually believe I might be a gold-digger?"

"No," he said confidently. Then he smiled. "At least not up to this point. But we'll see," he added, and they laughed.

Marti was laughing, but it was still a serious issue for her. "Every man I've ever been with were never satisfied with one woman. They were all cheats. They were all unfaithful to me. Every last one of them." Then she stared at him. "Are you like that too?"

Grant hated to admit it, but he wasn't going to lie to her. "Yes," he said.

Marti's heart dropped. Not another one! What was she thinking???

"Until I met you," Grant added, rubbing the side of her face with the back of his large hand.

When he said those words, Marti stared

at him. She studied him. She so wanted it to be true, but how could it be already? "How can you say that," she asked him, "when you've just met me?"

Grant stared at her. He was studying her too. "Sometimes you just know. Sometimes your heart tells you so."

Marti wanted to hear him say it. "And what is your heart telling you?" she asked him.

"My heart is telling me," Grant said as he placed his hand on the side of her smooth, gorgeous face, "that you could be the one. That you *are* the one."

Marti smiled that smile that melted his heart.

"What is your heart telling you?"

"*Girrl, get away from that joker and get away now!*"

Grant was alarmed.

Then Marti burst into laughter. "I'm playing with you boy!" she said, and Grant laughed too, grabbed her, and began tickling her.

Then they looked into each other's eyes. And the laughter turned into a look of serious affection. And they kissed. Until the fire between them almost consumed them, and they had to have more.

Grant entered her, and took her breath

away.

They made slow and rhythmic love. They weren't trying to rush it. For nearly an hour they rocked and they kissed and they shook and they slowed back down and they made the kind of love that made them know that they were on the right path.

And when they came, they came together. As if they were synchronized lovers. As if they were already together as one.

And for the second time in as many days, Grant slept like a baby all the way through the night. No nightmares. No terrors. No waking up at three a.m. And Marti didn't even think about four years ago, nor did she cry herself to sleep.

When she woke up the next morning, and realized he had gone, she didn't panic at all. He wouldn't just leave her. Oddly enough, she was convinced of it. She turned over and looked for the note.

And she found it! On her nightstand. "*Eat breakfast*," it read, although she had forgotten to ask him why he was so obsessed with her eating breakfast. Then it read: "*Your ass better not be late*," which made her laugh. But when she saw that it was signed *With Love*, that was epic enough. He actually wrote the word love and directed it at her! But when she saw that he ended the note with, *Your Boyfriend, G*, her heart melted. It just melted. And her laughter turned to tears of joy.

She was so happy that she didn't know how to handle that kind of elation. She hadn't felt that way since she first fell in love with her ex-husband. And even that young love didn't feel this deep. And they were just getting started. Tears dropped from her eyes like rain. She'd never met a man like Grant before. She'd never fallen so hard so fast for any man the way she was falling for Grant, and she still didn't know why. He wasn't even her type. She always went for guys her age or younger, not older men. And a white guy? She had never been into white guys before. But there it was. She was in love and, apparently, so was he! She could have laid there forever basking in this new thing they were trying to pull together.

Until she realized what time it was, and what he said she'd better not do, and she hopped out of that bed to pull her own self together.

CHAPTER TWENTY-THREE

When Marti arrived at the station, walked past the busy squad room and began heading for Grant's office, she noticed that the door to RJ's office, which was midway to Grant's office, was slightly open. But when she saw that a woman was standing in front of his desk and Grant was standing behind his desk, she slowed her walk. And when she realized that the woman and Grant appeared to be in a heated conversation, she stopped walking altogether and waited. Did she continue to his office, or just wait there? She was supposed to report to him after all. But she quickly wondered what was she waiting for? This man had made love to her last night. He left her a note this morning where he called himself her boyfriend. Was this woman his *girlfriend*?

Wait my ass, Marti thought as she detoured to RJ's office. She felt she had every right to know what was going on. And she wasn't going to speculate about it or leap to conclusions or let him explain it to her and put his own spin on it. She was going to find out for herself.

As she got closer, her heart began to pound and she didn't feel as confident anymore. She could tell the woman was drop-dead gorgeous. Tall and statuesque and all the rest: she had it going on. And she was talking like a woman seriously scorned, but in an upper-class, controlled angry voice. But her voice was too light for Marti to make out what she was actually saying. But her heart began hammering when she heard Grant yell, "*And you bring this shit to my police department? Are you out of your mind? You knew what the arrangement was, and you knew it from the beginning!*" He was talking as if they *still* had an arrangement. As if that woman was still in his stable of women. Did she get notes after he made love to her too???

Marti already felt that she had made a big mistake allowing her heart to even begin to get wrapped up in this man. He'd already told her he was a confirmed player just like all those other men she'd been with. What was she thinking???

She knocked lightly on the slightly opened door and then pushed it further open.

Grant was standing behind RJ's desk and Celeste, the woman that stood in front of

211

his desk, was blocking his view. When he leaned to his side to see who had knocked on RJ's door and saw that it was Marti, his heart squeezed with an anxiety he'd never had before. He didn't want her involved in his messiness! Not this early in their relationship. But he also knew Celeste was hellbent on airing their dirty laundry in public for all to see, and she was always the type that got what she wanted. He was pissed with her and wasn't thinking about her ass in the way she wanted him to think about her, but he didn't want Marti involved in this at all.

"Am I interrupting something?" Marti asked with that look of sincere curiosity on her face she couldn't conceal.

But when she heard that it was a woman's voice that had entered RJ's office, Celeste quickly turned around, her blonde hair bouncing as she turned. She looked Marti up and down as if she knew Marti had what it took to be her number one rival even though she'd never even met her. And just seeing Marti seemed to anger her even more.

She quickly turned back to Grant. "Is she the reason? Is this bitch the reason?"

Marti wanted him to shout *yes! Tell her I'm the reason*, but Grant didn't seem to want to give either one of them that satisfaction.

"Is she the reason, you bastard!" Celeste yelled again at him and then she picked up a file from RJ's desk and threw it at him.

"Okay that's it!" Grant angrily hurried from behind his captain's desk, grabbed Celeste by her skinny arm, and all but flung her out of that office. Fighting against his pull all the way, Celeste reached out her long leg and attempted to kick Marti, as if Marti was the problem, but Marti backed away from her reach.

"He's gonna do you the same way, sweetie," Celeste spat out at her. "Don't you think you're immune from this shit because we all thought that. He'll treat you just like he's treating me now! See how he's treating me? You bastard!" she cried out at Grant. "Leave me alone! You bastard!"

But Grant showed no compassion. She tried to hold onto the doorjamb, but he snatched her hands away and pushed her on out of RJ's office and then slammed the door shut.

It was only then, when the door slammed shut, did Marti realized that RJ was actually seated in his own office, along with Pete Kerrigan and Sergeant Carter too. She had been so focused on that woman and Grant and their relationship that she didn't even see them sitting there. And all three of them seemed bemused by what they'd just witnessed, as they glanced at each other, as if that woman's pain and the whole display was nothing new to them. And Grant was their hero because of his antics with women. Those were the kind of cops they were. Her heart was at stake here, and she was terrified that she just might get it broken by their so-called hero, by this man she was falling so deeply in love with, but they were behaving as if it was all a humorous game.

Grant and Marti exchanged a look that revealed what they both were seeing in the other one. Grant saw pain and anguish and concern on Marti's face. Marti saw embarrassment on Grant's face. And she could tell he wanted no parts in explaining it or justifying his actions or any of it. He just wanted to move the hell on. "Have a seat," he said to her and offered her a seat on the sofa.

Marti needed answers. She wanted answers. But not around RJ and gang. It was none of their damn business. As Grant went back and sat down behind the desk, Marti sat on the sofa.

Grant looked at the file that Celeste had scattered around RJ's office, and it displeased him that she had behaved as if she was entitled to him. "Want me to get it up?" he asked RJ.

RJ had a smirk on his handsome face. "Yeah, Chief, I want you to get it up," he said, and Pete and Carter laughed. "Please clean up your woman's mess."

When he said *your woman*, Marti glanced at Grant. But he didn't glance at her. And his men kept the joke going. "You're asking our chief to do manual labor?" asked Pete. "*Our* chief? Don't bet on it!"

RJ laughed. "I won't." And they laughed again.

But Marti could see that Grant was super-serious. He wasn't able to be playful like them. He was very playful around her, but never in public she noticed. Especially after such a very private display had been heaped upon a very private man.

He got down to business. "What were we talking about?" he asked them.

"You mean before we were so rudely interrupted?" asked Pete as he and RJ glanced at Marti as if *she* was the interruption.

"We were talking about the video from the shooting at Karney's," said Carter. "We were talking about that woman in that green pantsuit."

"Did you see what I meant?" asked Grant.

They all nodded. "That shooter was definitely eyeing her," said RJ. "I was amazed I didn't see it the first time."

"Thank our consultant for her eagle eye," said Grant. "She's the one that pointed it out to me. I missed it too."

Marti could tell none of Grant's men wanted to give her credit for anything, and that was fine by her. She wasn't thinking about them anyway. She was thinking about that woman and how Grant was going to handle her and the rest of his *stable* going forward. Or if he was going to handle them at all. What if he planned to keep them exactly as they were in his life? Something Marti was never going to allow herself to be a part of.

"What we need to do is get more intel on that lady in green," said RJ, "and what connection did she have to those two shooters at Karney's."

"Get a couple of guys on it," said Grant to RJ. "But not just her connection to the Karney shooters, but if she had a connection to the Wafer House shooter as well."

"I'll handle it," RJ said and as he was saying it the desk phone buzzed and Grant answered it.

"He's just taking over your desk, Cap," Carter said to RJ with a grin.

"Tell me about it," RJ said.

"What is it?" Grant said into the intercom.

"They said you were in Cap's office, sir," the clerk on the intercom said. "I had to tell him where you were."

Grant frowned. "Tell who?"

"Mayor Rickter is in the building and he's heading your way, sir."

"Shit!" said Grant and ended the conversation. He did not want to be bothered with Dooney's antics today.

"Why would he come all the way down here again?" asked Pete.

"Probably about yesterday," said RJ. "The public's very angry with the police department for not doing everything in our power to keep that shooter alive. They're convinced the two shootings are related and he could have reassured them that there's no network of mass shooters out there looking to do it again. He was mega-pissed that we turned his public relations triumph into a nightmare yesterday. He's still pissed."

"He keeps talking about how Governor Devere's holds grudges against him," said Carter. "Looks like he holds grudges against everybody else."

Marti sat upright. She knew the mayor didn't like her and she didn't like him. But she was going to keep her composure as the door to the office flew open and Mayor Dooney Rickter walked in. "Why aren't you in your office?" he said to Grant without looking at anybody else.

Grant remained cool behind the desk. "I didn't know that was a requirement."

"Fuck you, McGraw! Always got something smart to say. And fuck the BOBs for saddling me with you!"

"What do you want, Dooney?" Grant asked with irritation in his voice. "Or is yelling at me the goal?"

"That gal you wanted to kick my ass because you said I was disrespecting her," Dooney said, " just disrespected all of us."

Grant wanted to look at Marti, because he could see her from his side vision staring at the mayor as she had to be wondering what on earth he was yapping about, but he kept it together. "What are you talking about?" he asked the mayor.

"That chick sent a report to Tallahassee that excoriated every one of us."

"*Whaat*?" said a shocked RJ.

"If I didn't have connections in the AG's

office I wouldn't have even found out what was going on. And it's bad. She didn't hold back. They're already talking about shutting us down after just that one report! And that was before that debacle yesterday. That black bitch trying to bring us down!"

"Knock it off," Grant warned the mayor as RJ quickly cleared his throat. And it wasn't because he was black, too, but because he wanted to alert the mayor that the bitch he was referencing was in the office with them. When the mayor looked his way, he slyly pointed across the room.

When a still-angry Dooney looked across the room and saw Marti sitting there, he frowned. "What are you doing in here? Get out of here! Don't you see me having a meeting with my men? You'd better get your--"

Grant stood up. "That's enough, Dooney!" he warned again. But he understood his anger. He looked at Marti. "Wait in my office," he ordered her.

Marti wanted to rise up at that mayor and tell him about his butt, but she knew she'd be out of line. And besides, she could see that Grant was just as angry with her as the mayor. But he knew how to camouflage it better. "Yes, sir," she said and left the office.

But she felt sick to her stomach as she

went into Grant's office and took a seat on the sofa. She leaned her head back and fought back tears. It had been that kind of morning. First one of his ladies was giving him grief, probably for not returning her phone calls or whatever, and now that racist mayor was letting him know that her very first report wasn't flattering in the least about his department. And she had to own that shit because it was the truth.

But it was a day that was going nothing like she had expected it to go. It started out so promising. He wrote the word love in his note. He referred to himself as her boyfriend. It meant a lot to her. But to go from that to this shitshow? It seemed as if their affair was doomed to crash before it got off the ground. And she had been so hopeful!

CHAPTER TWENTY-FOUR

It would be over twenty-five minutes before Grant finally made his way into his office. The way he was looking at her as he closed the door told her everything she had feared was true: He was just as pissed with her as was the mayor.

He walked over to the sofa and sat beside her. She hadn't even noticed that once again his suit was pristine, his beautiful hair was well-groomed, and his bright-blue eyes were clear. He looked even more gorgeous than he'd ever had to her. It was like twisting the knife.

When he sat on the sofa, he leaned all the way back and folded his legs. She was seated upright on the edge of her seat because that was how she felt: on the edge.

"You sent in a report already?"

"Yes, but it was before we had . . ." She almost said the word *sex*, but she couldn't pull herself to go there. He looked so upset with her that that might make it worse.

"Why would you send a report already?" he asked her, his handsome face in a fixed frown as if he didn't understand her at all.

221

"When I fired my weapon at the Karney shooting, I had to file a report. It was standard procedure. And part of the report was to give my impressions of what was going on."

"Dooney said it was scathing. Was it?"

Marti didn't want to go there, but she was going to own what she wrote. "Yes."

"About the mayor and my department?"

"Yes."

"About me?"

She frowned as well. She hated to admit it. "Yes."

Grant was never a man who gave a damn what people thought about him, but he gave a damn what she thought about him. "What did you say about me and my department?"

"What I've already told you to your face."

"Which is?" He needed to hear it directly from her.

"Your officers aren't well-trained," she said. "They leap to conclusions without doing any investigations."

She paused before adding, "You don't seem to be well-trained, either."

She hated to say it, but knew she had to because it was also in her report. "I made clear that it was my early observation that this entire department is very poorly run."

Grant let out a harsh exhale as he stared at her with a look that bordered on rage. But it wasn't rage. It was adject disappointment. In himself!

It took him several minutes, but he ultimately spoke up. "I let my men down," he said.

He said it in a way so heartfelt that she could feel his pain. She continued to stare back at him.

"Because you're right," he said. "I don't know what I'm doing. But I keep doing it because it gives me something to live for. To hold onto. Even if I'm choking the life out of everybody under my command." He could see the pity in her eyes. "And don't tell me it's not my fault because it is."

"Yes, it is your fault," Marti agreed. She was never going to whitewash that kind of truth. "But you can get better. You have to."

Grant looked at her. He never felt more vulnerable in his entire life. "Will you help me get better?" he asked her.

It warmed Marti's heart. And she smiled. "You bet cha," she said, causing him to smile too.

She leaned back, against him, and he wrapped an arm around her.

They stayed that way for nearly a

quarter of an hour until his office door burst open and RJ hurried in.

Marti attempted to move away from Grant really quickly when RJ walked in, but Grant hesitated before releasing her. As if he didn't give a shit with appearances anymore. "What now?" he asked his captain.

"That report leaked to the media," RJ said.

"Who leaked it?" Grant asked him, upset."

"I'm willing to bet it came out of the AG's office."

"It had to," Marti agreed. "They're the only ones who would have that level of access."

RJ grabbed the TV's remote control from off of Grant's desk. "It's all over the media already," he said as he pressed on the TV that sat on the wall.

They watched as the breaking news report referred to it as a *scathing indictment* of the BPD. "A police consultant's report doesn't hold back," an anchorwoman was saying on the TV, "as she decimated the BPD for their incompetence at every level. She was especially brutal to Chief McGraw and Mayor Rickter."

Grant got up, snatched the remote from

RJ and turned the television off. He ordered him out of his office. "That's all you got time to do? Get back to work!"

RJ began leaving, but not before giving Marti a nasty look.

Grant exhaled and pulled out his keys. "Go to your hotel room," he said to her, "and pack your bags."

Marti stood up. "Why?"

"You'll be safer at my place," he said as he removed his house key from his chain of keys.

But Marti frowned as she walked over to him. "Safer? What do you mean?"

"What do you think I mean? You think they're going to take this shit lying down?"

"What shit?"

"That report!" He reached his key out to her. "Just do what I told you to do. Pack your bags and get to my house. They won't bother you there."

"I can take care of myself, Grant. And you don't even want anybody at your house."

"You aren't anybody. Now take this key," he said. "Go to my house and park in my garage. You'll find the button overhead inside the car." But when she continued to resist, he was blunt: "It's an order, not a suggestion."

She didn't like the implications of it. It

felt as if she was running away. Besides, how would it look to her bosses in Tallahassee if it ever got back to them that she was staying with the man that she was there to observe?

But she saw that concern in Grant's eyes. This was the big leagues. He wasn't playing. "Yes sir," she said and took the key.

They stared at each other longer, with both of them feeling as if their relationship didn't stand a chance, and then she walked out of his office.

But she wasn't gone ten seconds before RJ was walking back in.

"Didn't I tell you to get back to work?" Grant began walking behind his desk, although his voice sounded drained.

"We're fucked if the state takes over," RJ said. "You're out the door and probably all of us right along with you. All because of that bitch."

Grant hurried back around his desk and jacked RJ up and ran with him until he slammed him against his file cabinet. "You and your lapdogs had better stay away from her," he warned RJ, "or you'll answer to me. Do I make myself clear, Captain?"

RJ frowned. "Man, she really got you twisted around. She that good in bed?"

The chief slammed him against that file

cabinet again. "Do I make myself clear?" he yelled at him.

"Yes!" RJ yelled back, in pain. "Damn. Yes sir!"

"And call her bitch again and you'll become my bitch," Grant added.

"Yes sir!" RJ said again, but even louder.

Then the chief, realizing how unhinged he was, let his captain go. And RJ straightened his suit as if he was the one in control, and left the office.

Grant leaned his head back and closed his weary eyes. He couldn't even begin to unpack how devastated he felt on every turn. But especially about his relationship with Marti.

CHAPTER TWENTY-FIVE

It was nightfall by the time he made it home. But he didn't go in right away. Because it felt strange. There was his house, at night, with the downstairs lit up like a Christmas tree. Lights on everywhere. Even the porch light was on, something he never had any reason to turn on. Somebody was in his home. He had actually invited her in. And he wasn't at all sure how he felt about such a dramatic shift in his lifestyle.

And what transpired today, first with Celeste and then with that report, didn't help his mood either.

After a few minutes of just sitting there, he finally went inside.

The first thing that hit him was the smell. The smell of food. And not just any food, but very wonderful-smelling food.

"That you?"

It was Marti's voice coming from his kitchen.

"Yes, it's me," he yelled back.

"I'm in the kitchen!"

He saw his mail sitting on his foyer table as he sat his keys and briefcase down. She had gone down to the end of his driveway and got his mail out of the box. He didn't know how he felt about that either.

He grabbed the mail and thumbed through it as he made his way to his kitchen. He could tell a difference as he walked through his own home. The entire space looked brighter and airier to him. Cleaner. He went into the kitchen.

As soon as he turned the corner from the dining hall and saw Marti at the stove, her back to him, he stopped in his tracks. She wore shorts and a cut-off t-shirt and her hair hung down her back in waves of curls. He stood there staring at her. And just from that view alone, his heart warmed to her. And when she turned around to look at him, and he saw those big, creamy brown eyes, his heart just melted. He loved her. That was what compelled him to place that word on that note earlier that morning. Because he loved her. He leaned against the archway that led into his big, gourmet kitchen. There was no getting around it.

He remembered what his mother told him years ago when he asked why she stayed with his father, who cheated on her every day of their marriage. *"You can't help who you love,"* she said to him. *"Don't fool yourself."*

Hey," he said to Marti.

Marti was smiling, but when she saw how exhausted he looked her heart went out to him. "You look so tired, Grant," she said as she removed the pot from the gas burner and turned it off. She began walking to him. "You look like you can barely stand up."

She wanted to hug him, but she wasn't sure if he was still pissed with her. So she didn't initiate it.

Grant wanted her in his arms, too, but he didn't know if she had reached a different conclusion than he had. He loved her was the conclusion he had reached. No matter what. Did she reach the totally opposite conclusion? "What are you cooking?"

"I'm baking some salmon with roasted potatoes and collard greens."

"Wow. That sounds delicious."

"Want me to run you a bath? I think if you soak in the tub for a little while it can refresh you."

That sounded like a brilliant idea to Grant. "Yes, I think that will help. But you don't have to do it. I can manage."

"I don't mind," Marti said with a smile. "I just don't know which room is yours. I checked out the rooms downstairs, but none of those looked lived-in, and I didn't feel comfortable enough to go upstairs."

Grant touched her arm. "You can go anywhere you want to go in this house. No space is off limits, you hear me? You can go anywhere."

Marti nodded. He always looked so sincere about the littlest thing. "Okay. Thank you."

Then she smiled again as he just stood there staring at her. "Lead the way," she said, and it appeared only then did he realize that he needed to show her where his room was located.

"Where did you put your things?" he asked her as they began walking out of the kitchen.

"In that first room off from the foyer," Marti said. "The first one I got to. I assumed it was a guest room."

"It is," Grant said. But instead of going upstairs where Marti assumed he was going to go, he went to the room she'd just mentioned. He placed his mail in his suit coat and grabbed the luggage she had sitting on the bed.

"What are you doing?"

"You're going to be upstairs with me," he said.

But Marti stopped his progression by moving in his path. They were face to face, within a few inches of each other. "Upstairs with you," she said, "but in my own room, right?"

He stood there staring at her. "Is that what you want?"

"That's what I need, yes," she said. "We still have things to work out before we go full bore." Then she stared deeply into his tired eyes. "Don't you think?"

He knew what she said was true. But he also knew she might be having loads of doubts about him. Which only made her statement even truer. "Yes," he said with a nod. "Upstairs with me, but in your own room."

She smiled, and he managed to return her smile. Then he led her upstairs to the master bedroom. It was a wow moment for Marti because his bedroom seemed larger than any she'd ever seen. "This is a lot," was all she could manage to say.

"The bathroom is in there," he said, pointing to her left.

"Can you show me to my room," she said, "then I can run your bath without bothering you afterwards."

"This is your room," Grant said as if it went without saying.

Marti knew this could not possibly be a guest room. "But this is *your* room," she said.

"Don't worry, I'm not going to intrude on your territory. I'll take one of the guest rooms up here. I have plenty."

"Yes, but, this is the master bedroom."

"That's correct."

"I don't want to take your room. A guest room is plenty for me."

"There's no way."

Marti was puzzled. "What do you mean there's no way?"

"You will sleep in the best room in this house always. And this is the best room in this house bar none. There's no way I'm sleeping better than you."

Marti found herself overwhelmed with emotion. For a man to give her the best he had was so new to her that it staggered her. And the tears appeared in her eyes.

When Grant saw those tears in her huge eyes, his heart melted again. And he dropped her bags and pulled her into his arms.

When she wiped her eyes with the handkerchief he provided to her, she pulled back and looked at him. He kept his arms around her waist. "Just thinking enough of me to invite me into your home when I know you don't do that was monumental for me. But to do this? To give me your best like this?" She shook her head as the tears began to return.

"You don't have to do this, Grant. You've done so much."

She was about to wipe her eyes again but he stopped her by grabbing her hand. "I haven't even scratched the surface. And don't you ever think I've ever done everything I can do for you because I don't think that's possible. Yes, we have things to work out. Yes, I'm sure you have your doubts. I have mine too," he said. "But don't ever doubt how I feel about you because I'm going to make that clear to you."

Marti was so happy when he said he could never do enough for her, but then she became confused and scared when he said he had doubts too. And then he said he was going to make himself clear to her. But make clear what? What was he going to make clear? Was he going to say he loved her, or that he didn't? Was he going to say their relationship stood a chance, or not any at all? Her entire body was suddenly a bundle of nerves.

Until he said those three words.

He placed his hands on both sides of the face he thought was the most adorable he'd ever faced. "I love you," he said with such conviction in his heart that it felt as if he'd known her a lifetime.

When those words came, all of those nerves drifted away and Marti's heart soared. "I love you, too, Grant," she said to him. "I love you too!" And they kissed a kiss that for the first time was more about their love for each other than just their lust.

But that didn't mean they didn't end up in bed. They did, after she had drawn Grant's bath, they bathed together, and after they had eaten her delicious dinner.

But first Grant caught her at her own game. They made their way upstairs, arm in arm, but when they got to the master bedroom, Grant didn't go inside. "Good night," he said to her, pecked her on her cheek, and then headed for the guest room where he was going to be staying.

He could tell she was still just standing there, probably confused, but he kept on walking and went to his room, removed his robe, and got in his bed. He was inwardly laughing all the way. Because he felt he knew her. Because he felt she wore her feelings on her sleeve and he could tell she was feeling the fire tonight.

And just as he had predicted, within minutes of their departure, he could hear his bedroom door creak open, he could hear her walking on the back side of his bed, and he could hear her get in his bed.

He turned around suddenly, holding his covers up to his bare chest. "What's the meaning of this?" he said as if she was there to violate him.

She looked puzzled. "But I thought," she began to say, worried that she had misread the room completely, until she could see he was unable to keep his composure and a smile broke through. And then great laughter. She hit him so hard that he thought she meant it. And then they both were laughing. And tickling each other.

And then, ultimately, back in the master bedroom in *their* bed now, they made love. Long, wonderful, passionate love.

But afterwards, when the euphoria had died down and it was just the two of them, side by side, staring into the darkness of the room, Marti had to ask it. "Who was that woman this morning?"

It wasn't as if he didn't expect the question to eventually come up. "Celeste," he said.

"That's her name, okay. But who is she to you?"

Grant exhaled. "A friend." Then he added, "Who used to have benefits."

"Used to have?" Marti looked at him.
He looked at her. "Yes."

"When did these benefits stopped?"

"Since I met you."

"But I mean how long before you met me did they stop?" In other words, she thought, when was the last time you slept with this Celeste? Given how angry she was, it had to be recently.

"A few days before," he admitted, although he would have rather not. But Marti was a smart girl. She knew what questions to ask.

"That's what I call the ink not yet dry for her," Marti said.

"For her. But it's bone-dry for me."

Marti could have smiled, but somebody else's loss and pain, because she could tell Celeste loved Grant, wasn't something she was going to celebrate. "Is that a part of this?"

Grant didn't follow her. "A part of what? You and me?"

"The fact that you said for my safety you wanted me to stay at your house?"

Grant stared at her. "No. This has nothing to do with that."

"Then who should I fear if not one of your scorned women? Because I'm sure there's more to come."

Grant knew it too. "I just didn't want any rogue cop to think they could take any liberties with you and try, under the guise of their badge, to harass you because of that report. That's what I meant."

"Is there anyone in particular I should be concerned about?"

"None of them. I've personally spoken to all of the principals to notify their underlings who might think they're doing their boss's bidding by harassing you."

Marti was touched. "You've spoken to all of them on my behave?"

"Yes."

"They don't view you as a traitor?"

Grant hadn't even thought about that. "I don't care if they do or not," he said. "Changes have got to be made. And it's going to begin with me."

Marti smiled, kissed him, and then cuddled up against him. They interlaced their fingers.

"Bet you can't go another round," he said to her.

Marti looked at him. He had the libido of a teenager! "No more rounds," she said, shutting it down for the night. "You need your rest."

Grant smiled, because she was so right.

And once again, they both slept the sleep of two truly happy people. It was a remarkable turnaround for two lonely, tortured souls.

But they couldn't be anything but who they were. And because they were so unaccustomed to peace and happiness that they couldn't help but wait for, depend on, peep around corners looking for, the next shoe to drop.

CHAPTER TWENTY-SIX

Three weeks later and it was still going good. No shoes were trying to drop and they were beginning to appreciate their new, happier lot in life. And all that talk of separate bedrooms flew out the window that first night in Grant's home when they slept together. They'd been sleeping together, in peace and harmony, ever since. And Grant was still leaving Marti his usual notes. And they all contained that one same proviso: eat breakfast.

But when Marti saw it this time, she realized she still had not asked him why. After getting up, bathing and dressing and hopping in her car, backing out of his garage, and making her way to work, she decided to phone and asked him. She always forgot to bring it up when they were together. She was determined to bring it up this time. Especially since she was leaving too late for breakfast.

"Hey." He had been at work for over three hours already.

"Why do you always put that in your note?"

"Put what in my note?"

240

"For me to eat breakfast."

"Because I know you don't eat breakfast."

"How would you know that? You're always gone when I wake up, and we haven't known each other *that* long. How would you know my eating patterns?"

"Because you're small. And I don't want you to get any smaller. I told you I want meat on your bones."

"But I'm not skinny."

"I didn't say you were skinny," Grant said, "but if you keep missing meals you will be."

Marti smiled as she turned into the McDonald's parking lot. "I thought you liked skinny women."

"Why would you think that? I said just the opposite."

"Celeste is skinny."

"Celeste isn't my woman. She's somebody I used to sleep around with. You aren't in that category."

"But you sleep around with me."

"I do not *sleep around* with you. I sleep with you. That's different."

Marti smiled again. "If you say so," she said doubtfully. Then she added: "Let me place my order."

"Where are you?"

"McDonald's. I'm grabbing a coffee. The coffee at the office sucks."

"Grab an Egg McMuffin while you're at it."

"I don't like Egg McMuffins."

"Do it, Marti."

Marti rolled her eyes.

"May I help you?" It was the woman on the drive through intercom.

"Yes, ma'am, I'll take a coffee with two sugars, no cream, and an Egg McMuffin."

The woman gave her the total, and she drove past the order window and waited in line.

"And make sure you eat it," Grant said.

"I'll try. Eating this early in the morning ain't my thing."

"Eating any time of the day doesn't seem to be your thing. Just do it. But anyway, I've got to go," he said, and then he just ended the call.

After paying for and retrieving her order, she got back on the highway to make her way to the station. But the way he abruptly ended their call after barking out orders to her was beginning to concern her. He always did that to her. And he way he insisted she order food she didn't even like concerned her too. Sometimes he came across as if he knew what

242

was best for her even if she disagreed with him. It was as if he was in complete control of their relationship. A relationship that was solidly under wraps, not just at work, but around town too. She couldn't even park her car on his driveway. She always had to put it in his garage. And whenever they sat outside on his gorgeous front porch, it was always late at night. They had no dinner dates out. No movie nights. Just the two of them inside his house. Which was fine for now. Their affair was still young. But eventually she was going to want more.

And ever since that night he told her that he loved her, he hadn't said it again. They'd talk on the phone and when he was ready for the call to end, he'd just end it. No *love you, bye*, or not even just *bye*. He hung up. And Marti was allowing it. But only because she so wanted this relationship to work! Even though, if she was to be truthful with herself, none of her past affairs worked out despite her best efforts because of the cheating. They were all cheaters. All of them. That was the level of man she always picked, and always ended up losing herself over.

Grant isn't that kind of man, she reminded herself as she made her way to town. But she would have never thought

Roger was that kind of man, either, or Dexter or Mikey or Lawrence or any of the others that came before. And also like them, Grant was domineering. He was a control freak. She knew that the moment she met him. And it was beginning to look very familiar to her because all of her priors were control freaks too. But Grant's control always centered around helping her. Doing for her. Paying attention to her. What he thought was best for her. The men in her prior relationships were all about her catering to them and being there for them and doing for them. It was all about them. Grant was all about her. That was what separated him from them.

BAM!

She heard the crash before she felt it. Then she felt the tail end of her Charger lifting up and then slamming back onto the street. She quickly looked through her rearview mirror and saw one of those huge four-door pickup trucks ramming into her car again, causing her car to swerve so recklessly that it nearly swerved out of control.

But she regained control, realized that this was no accidental crash, and put her pedal to the metal. She floored it and sped away.

But the fact that the back of her Charger was dragging in the street, creating sparks and fire, slowed her tremendously. She couldn't take off the way she wanted to and that massive pickup was able to stay on her tail and ram her again.

But when she was able to control the swerve such that she only went side to side briefly, and as they were approaching an intersection, the driver of the big truck apparently lost patience and sped up beside her car and attempted to perform a PIT maneuver on Marti's car.

But Marti was a cop to her soul. She knew how to perform PITs, and she knew how to avoid them too. She avoided the first one, as she moved side to side to prevent that truck from slamming the side of her automobile.

But as she entered the intersection and was forced to run the redlight or be killed by that big truck, she suddenly had to slam on brakes when another car, who had the green light, was flying through the intersection. She avoided the car because the car saw her and swerved out of her way, but the truck was able to slam into the side of Marti's Charger with such force that she found herself spinning in the middle of a busy intersection.

Most of the cars were able to stop from hitting her. But one car, driven by a texting teen, slammed into her mid-spin and both of

them went careening across the divide until
they both ended up in the ditch. People,
horrified by what they'd witnessed and how
close it nearly took them out, too, hopped out
of their vehicles and ran to assist the two
drivers.

But the driver of the pickup truck that
had been tormenting Marti before that crash,
turned left at that intersection, and kept going.

CHAPTER TWENTY-SEVEN

"Don't even try it, Pete," RJ joked. "You and your ball-and-chain will be at that ball just like the rest of us."

"Why you always calling my wife a ball and chain as if yours ain't?" Pete asked his Commanding Officer.

"My wife knows I run our household. Your wife don't know that shit," RJ said and they all laughed. "Your wife wears the pants in that bitch."

"You don't know what you're talking about. She doesn't even wear pants."

"See what I mean?" said RJ. "She's so big and bad she can lord it over you in a housedress." They all laughed again.

They were in Grant's office for his morning meeting with all of the senior staff, and as usual Grant wasn't laughing. His meeting with his patrol officers didn't go so well. They were complaining about the public still hounding them about how they bungled those mass shooting investigations and still hadn't told them anything definitively. They were blaming all the cops, not the shooters themselves, and not just the cop that shot the shooter they had in custody. They were blaming everybody. And Grant didn't know what to tell them.

But that was why he was watching his television as he studied that video from the shooting at Karney's grocery store. His men were joking around. Grant wanted to find answers.

"Why we always got to go to the mayor's ball every year anyway, Chief?" Carter asked him. "I don't like being around them uppity mucks like that."

"Neither do I," said RJ.

But they all laughed. "Quit lying, Cap," Carter said. "You fit right in. You're the mayor's boy."

RJ gave Carter a hard look. "Who you calling a boy, boy?" he said. There was a tense moment. Grant even glanced at RJ. Then RJ cracked that smile again Grant's men laughed at that too.

But Grant replayed that video.

RJ noticed it. "When are you going to give it a rest?"

"When we figure out why we had two mass shootings in one week when we never had any mass shootings in the history of this town. That's when I'll give it a rest."

"Is that consultant filling your head with all that stuff?" Pete asked. "Talk about a ball-and-chain, she's been following you around all day long like she's your shadow for the past three weeks. Even after her vicious report came out. Like she has no shame about it. I would have told her to keep her ass out of my sight after what she wrote in that report."

"That's what I'm saying," RJ agreed.

But Grant wasn't mixing it up with them over Marti. She was off limits. "What's the deal on those other ladies holed up in that office with the shooter? What did we find out about them?"

"The lady in green is a hair stylist in town with a lot of boyfriends," RJ said, "but we couldn't find any connection whatsoever between her and any of the three shooters. Including the shooter holed up in that office with her. We told you that three weeks ago, Chief."

"I'm not talking about her. I'm talking about the other females in that office with her and the shooter. Before he opened fire on them, yes, he looked at the lady in green. But maybe that was on purpose too."

They all looked at their chief. "What do you mean?"

"Maybe him staring at her was a way to

keep us from seeing who the real target was."

"*What?*" RJ voiced all of their sentiments because they all found the chief's suggestion ludicrous. "Why would he do all of that subterfuge?"

"He had to know a camera was in that office," said Grant. "It's worth pursuing."

"Says who?" asked Pete. "That consultant?"

Grant had had it with his disrespect. "You will refer to her as Lieutenant Nash. You hear me? I already told you that."

As usual when Grant bothered to assert his authority, they always backed down. "Yes sir."

"Get more detectives on the case to look into it," Grant ordered RJ as his office door opened and an officer peered inside.

"What is it?" RJ asked. They hated being interrupted during their morning meeting.

"Sorry to disturb you, sir," the officer said to Grant.

"Then don't disturb him," said Pete.

"We just got word, sir," the officer continued, staring only at Grant, "that Lieutenant Nash has been in a car crash."

As soon as Grant heard her name and the words car crash, he jumped up from his seat so fast that he knocked his chair over.

Everybody in that office seemed surprised. "A car crash?"

"Yes sir."

Grant was grabbing his coat and hurrying toward his door. "Is she alright?" His heart was pounding.

"We don't know the full extent of her injuries yet, sir. She's been transported to Marymount. All we know is that other vehicles were involved, one of which was a hit-and-run driver, and that her car was totaled."

Totaled? Grant's heart was hammering as he gave a hard look at RJ and Pete.

RJ was offended. "It wasn't us!" he said forcefully.

Grant would kick their asses later if it was, but all he could think about in that moment was getting to Markita. He ran out of his office.

"Do you want me to drive you, sir?" Sergeant Carter was yelling after him, but Grant was gone.

"Damn," said Pete. "What's with that? You'd think it was his child or somebody like that who was in that car crash."

"And for him to look at us like we did it," said Carter. "We hate the bitch, true enough, but he's got some nerve."

"Let's just get back to work," ordered RJ

and they all stood up. "I'll find out what I can and give an update."

"You don't have to update me," said one of the senior staff as they walked out of the chief's office.

"I couldn't care less," said another.

But when they all had gone, Pete, who hung back, looked at RJ. "Was it us?" he asked him.

RJ smiled. "The best misdirection ever!"

Pete was confused. What did he mean? He never seemed to know where RJ was coming from. But as long as RJ knew what was going on, Pete was okay with it. He smiled too.

CHAPTER TWENTY-EIGHT

The automatic doors of the Marymount Baptist Hospital of Belgrave, Florida flew open and Grant was met by a gaggle of reporters and photographers hanging out in the lobby as microphones were shoved in his face and camera lights were flicking in his eyes.

A nurse was waiting for him. "This way, Chief," she said promptly as they began hurrying down the hall. The reporters were following them.

"Why are they allowed in here?" Grant asked her as they hurried.

"It's a public space. They aren't allowed beyond these doors, however," she said as they hurried toward the inner doors.

But as they were hurrying, the press didn't hesitate to lob questions their way.

"Chief, why would you here to check on a consultant that called you and your department incompetent?"

"She has nothing but contempt for you."

"How did you feel when she questioned your ability to run the police department, sir? Were you angry with her, sir?"

"Did you have something to do with her car accident, Chief?"

Grant gave a chilling look to the reporter that asked that ridiculous question as the nurse pressed the big button on the side of the wall and the double doors opened. He was able to escape any further ridiculousness. He hurried to Marti's bedside.

Fearing that it was going to be a repeat of his sister's Dana's plight in the hospital, he hesitated before walking into her room. He didn't know what he was going to see. But when he finally got up the strength to walk on in, he was relieved to see that Marti wasn't even in bed. She had just taken off her hospital gown and was about to put on her bra when Grant walked in without bothering to knock. When the nurse, who was behind him, saw the state of her patient, she tried to block Grant. But Grant hurried around her and rushed to Marti. As soon as Marti saw him, too, she dropped her bra and fell into his opened arms.

The nurse, stunned by what she was seeing between their police chief and the police consultant, quickly realized more was at work here than a professional relationship. She discreetly backed out of the room and closed the door.

Grant, so relieved and delighted that he was near tears, pulled back and looked Marti squarely in the eyes. "Were you hurt anywhere?"

"No, thank God. I wasn't harmed at all. But the teenager in the car that hit me was. She'll survive, but the doctor said she was banged up pretty badly." Then she looked at Grant. "It wasn't an accident."

"You think that teenager hit you on purpose?"

"Not her. But whoever was driving the truck."

Grant was confused. "What truck?"

"A big four-door pickup truck rammed me from behind and tried to PIT me, but I was able to escape him. Until I got in that intersection and had to slam on brakes. That's when he hit me again. That's when I lost control."

"And then he took off?"

She nodded. "From what I've been told, yes. He took off."

Grant pulled her in his arms again. If he found out it was any of his guys involved, he was going to kill them before he fired them. He was just that angry.

"What if," she started to say but stopped.

Grant pulled back from her again. "What if what?"

"When you moved me into your house, you said I would be safer there because you didn't want some rogue cop harassing me. Was that really what you were concerned about?"

"A part of it, yes."

"What was the other part?"

"I have guys on the force who don't want the band dismantled. You could dismantle the band. They may go to great lengths to keep the band together. That's the other part. But mainly I was worried about the harassment more than anything else."

"But maybe they decided to do more than harass me."

"Maybe. I doubt it, but we'll see," he said, and held her again.

She felt warm and protected in his arms. "They wanted to keep me overnight and run all kinds of tests," she said as he held her, "but I told them I was fine. I told them I'm not staying overnight in any hospital."

When Grant heard that, he pulled back from her. "They want to run tests?"

"Yes. But I told them I'm not going for that."

"Oh yes you are," Grant said firmly.

"They'll run every test they need to run to make certain you're okay. What's wrong with you?" He seemed angry. "You can have internal injuries you don't even know about and you don't wanna find out if you do or not? To hell with that!"

"But I hate hospitals, Grant."

"Tough. Put back on that gown."

"Grant!"

"I'm not playing with you, Markita. Put it on!"

"There you go again," Marti said, "bossing me around."

But Grant gave her a look that made debating the issue a nonstarter. He was not backing down.

A part of her knew he was right. She could have internal injuries. But she hated hospitals!

But when she didn't move fast enough for him, Grant grabbed that hospital gown and put it back on her himself. Then he informed the staff that she wasn't going anywhere. That she was ready to take any test they wanted to give to her, and he wanted them to give her all they had. He would foot the bill.

The charge nurse, pleased by this new development, notified the doctor.

CHAPTER TWENTY-NINE

That Friday night and they were heading to the mayor's annual ball. Marti didn't think she was going to be able to attend anything four days ago. Those doctors ordered so many x-rays and lab work that she was certain they were bound to find something was wrong with her. But they didn't find a thing. Late that next evening, she was free to leave the hospital. She was glad Grant had ordered her to stay.

But going to a ball wasn't something she was accustomed to, especially going to a ball that a mayor who hated her guts was hosting. But he invited her to quell any public speculation about his hatred of her, Grant had purchased her a gorgeous ball gown, and she agreed to go. She was at least getting out for a change.

Which surprised her too. "Aren't you worried?" she asked him as he drove them to the mayor's mansion.

Grant glanced at her. "Worried about what?"

"When you show up with me by your side. I'm sure Captain Jeffers and Lieutenant Kerrigan are expecting you to show up with Celeste or Ingrid or any number of those other ladies that constantly call your phone. But you're showing up with me."

"You or nobody," Grant said.

But Marti stared at him. "I thought our relationship was a secret."

"It was. It wasn't any of their business."

"But now it's their business?"

"No. It's ours. And I'm tired of hiding you. Hiding means it's wrong. What I was doing with all those other women was what was wrong. Being with you will never be wrong."

Marti smiled. It was those moments, when Grant could be so charming, that kept her from calling him out every time he took control of what should be *her* business. Because he was never petty with it. Like at the hospital earlier that week. He was never bossy for bossy sake. Or because he had it going on like that. It was all about what was best for her. And since he was older than her, and a wise man in many ways even though he was a lousy cop, she could dig what he was laying down. He wasn't like any of the others.

But she did have her limits.

Grant looked down at her beautiful red ball gown. "You look gorgeous by the way," he said to her.

She smiled a smile that brightened up the night.

"But be prepared," he warned her. "The knives will be out tonight."

Marti smiled. "These women don't scare me. But rogue cops do," she added, as her smiled dampened.

Grant took her hand. "I've got you covered," he said to her in a voice so reassuring that she believed him. He could do no wrong in her eyes, which, she knew, wasn't healthy. But it was their relationship right now.

He pulled up to the mayor's mansion on a regular street of other big houses, and drove around the curve where the valets were stationed.

Grant looked at Marti again. Marti exhaled. And then they got out of his Maybach.

CHAPTER THIRTY

The ball was festive from beginning to end. What Marti loved about Grant was that he tried his best to stay by her side, although he was constantly pulled away by one big wig after another one. They were all members of the Belgrave Oversight Board she'd heard about, and Grant introduced her to each one of them. Compared to the police staff and Mayor Rickter, the BOBs were very kind to her. And they seemed to genuinely respect Grant. They were actually a welcomed relief.

But it didn't take long for the sharks to start circling. Marti was walking around the room, doing all she could to avoid any contact with Mayor Rickter, when she ran into Celeste. And Celeste was not alone.

Marti heard her say *there she is,* and that was all it took. Four beautiful women, including Celeste, came tramping over.

"So you're the latest new thing," said the tallest woman of the group, presumably the leader.

Marti didn't dignify that comment with a response. She sipped her champagne.

"You're pretty, but so are we."

Another idiotic comment.

"What day are you?"

When Celeste asked that question, it did get Marti's attention. "What day am I?"

"Yes! We all have a day. Well, not technically, but he tends to answer my calls on certain days, but not on other days when he answers another one of his ladies' calls. It's just how he is. What day are you?"

Marti thought about Chaka Khan singing, *I'm Every Woman*, and smiled. "I'm every day," she said.

They laughed. "Yeah, we thought so too," said the tall drink of water.

"In the beginning," said Celeste, "we were every day as well. But that doesn't last long at all."

"Not at all," agreed another one of the ladies.

"It's always good in the beginning," Celeste continued. "But we all realized the truth in the end."

When she didn't continue, Marti was too curious. "Which is?"

"There is no way one woman can satisfy Grant McGraw."

"No way," said Stretch.

"No way," said another one, and they laughed.

But Marti saw through the laughter. She remembered how hurt Celeste was when Grant all but threw her out of his office. They all loved him. They all wanted him. They all, although they'd never admit it, wished they were in Marti's shoes. They wished they were the new thing all over again. That was why Marti couldn't pretend and join in the laughter. Because although they might have wished they were her, she, if she was to be honest with herself, was them. They'd been where she now was. Now they were has-beens. Was that where she was headed too?

They distressed her more than even running into the mayor could have. She just wanted out.

But she couldn't leave. They had to have dinner.

It came nearly an half hour later. She and Grant had been on the dance floor trying to enjoy all that Neil Sedaka kind of music the orchestra was playing. From *Laughter in the Rain* to *Breaking Up is Hard to Do*, all they played was that elevator music. But when he specifically asked them to play a song called *I'm a Song, Sing Me*, Marti was about to jump out of her skin. Ever hear of Beyonce? What about Mary J. Blige? Whitney *hello*? But Grant pulled her closer against him grinning, knowing how much she hated the music being played. And when he could tell she was really ready to let the orchestra have a piece of her mind, he whispered in her ear, trying to keep a straight face. "Don't you dare," he said to her, and they both grinned. Then it was time to eat.

They all sat around the one big table in the huge dining hall. All the senior police staff and other government officials sat around the table, with Mayor Rickter at the head of the table. But what shocked Marti the most was that every one of those ladies that had encircled her and proclaimed themselves to be among Grant's stable of women, were seated at that table beside their husbands. Their *husbands*!

She looked at Grant as if it had to be news to him too. She leaned against him. "They're married?" she asked him.

When he nodded as if it was no big thing, Marti was floored. *What kind of Peyton Place shit is this*, she wanted to scream out. Grant never told her he fooled around with married women. He never even mentioned it! And the way he was behaving like it was no big deal to him, worried Marti. What more, she wondered, was he keeping from her?

But when Grant saw that concerned look on her face as they ate, he placed his hand under the table and squeezed her thigh. When he got her attention, he leaned toward her and said, "I'm not them," as if that was all he needed to say.

But he just happened to be the one in the illicit relationships that wasn't married. But what if he did get married? Would he be just like them then? It was a question she was dying to ask Grant.

But she didn't get a chance until they were leaving the mayor's house, walking toward his car, and he was laughing.

"You manage to avoid Dooney all night long. It's a world record," he said and laughed.

But she was still reeling from his ladies. "You knew they were married?" she asked him.

Grant looked at her, and his smile slowly dissipated. They stopped walking. "Why are you making a big deal about that?"

"Because it is a big deal, Grant. How could you sleep with another man's wife? That's foul."

Grant looked at her. He could see the disappointment in her eyes. And he was ashamed. "I didn't want any attachments and neither did they. At least in the beginning," he added.

"But what about their husbands?"

"What about them? You think they're

innocents? They have their sidepieces too. It's the way it works in the upper echelons around here."

"But I'm against that, Grant. That goes against everything I believe it. I could never cheat on my husband and I could never stay with a man who cheats on me. I don't care how it works around here!"

"Lower your voice," Grant said when other couples that were standing outside started glancing over at them.

Marti settled down.

Grant stared at her. "I won't hurt you, Marti. And if we get married," he added, "I promise you'll never have to worry about that."

It wasn't lost on Marti that he said *if we get married* and not *when we get married*. And that little comment alone reminded her that nothing was set in stone with Grant. They were in a good place, but it was nothing to write home about. At least not yet. At least not for him. That feeling of being adrift began to capture her again.

Grant saw the change in her. "What's wrong?" he asked her. "You don't believe me?"

But as she thought about his question, his attention was drawn to a vehicle that had just arrived on the street. What made it appear out of place was the fact that among so many Mercedes and Bentleys and Porsches and Lamborghinis, it was this big, four-door pickup truck. A badly dented pickup truck at that. The same kind of truck Marti had described as slamming into her, and causing her to crash.

But just as he realized it might be the same truck, that very truck accelerated, jumped the curb, and raced across the mayor's front lawn so fast that Grant only had time to push Marti as far out of the path of that truck as quickly as he could and then to dive on top of her, to cover her. The truck flew by them, missing Grant's diving legs by a hare's breath, and then it crashed violently into the front brick of the mayor's mansion. People were screaming and scrambling to get out of the path of that truck too.

Grant got off of Marti, asking if she was okay. "I'm okay, I'm okay," Marti was nervously saying as he helped her on her feet. "Are you okay?"

"I wasn't struck," he said.

Marti frowned. "It looks like that same truck from my accident, Grant," she said to him, which confirmed his suspicion. He and Marti, along with the other cops out there, hurried to the truck, their guns drawn.

But the driver was slumped over the

steering wheel as dead as his engine. He was gone.

They all took a look at him, but none of them recognized him as anybody local. But Marti wasn't local, either, and when she leaned in to get a look at the deceased truck driver, her heart dropped.

Grant noticed the change. "You know him?" he asked her.

But she was still staring at him. And she was in shock. "*Eric*?" It sounded as if she was asking the dead man if he was whom he appeared to be.

"Who's Eric?" Grant asked her.

"Eric?" she asked the dead man again.

"Marti, who's Eric?" Grant asked her again.

"Eric Peterson. He's my friend. We knew each other for years. He was a very good friend of mine in Memphis. Why would he . . ." She could not believe it. She just couldn't.

Grant placed his arm around her as everybody stood around in a state of shock too. They couldn't believe something this crazy had happened. Even the mayor, who always had too much to say, had nothing to say. He stayed away from the carnage. But Marti was suffering on a different level. She actually knew the man who seemed to have been aiming directly for her. It was Eric. It was the same man upset that Andy Sloan had crashed her daughter's sweet sixteen party. Eric used to be her road dog. What happened???

But as Grant held her, and as everybody continued to stare at the wreckage, ambulances and more police officers began arriving.

The paramedics hurried over to make sure the driver of the pickup was a goner. He was, but they couldn't take anybody's word for it. Grant backed Marti away so they could do their job.

But Marti was still unable to process the reality of it. She looked at Grant. "We were really close. He was a great friend of mine. Why would he try to kill me?"

It was the question Grant was determined to answer. But he knew it wasn't going to happen tonight. He took her to his car and sat her on the front passenger seat.

He knew it would be protocol for them to wait until somebody other than him could question her about her knowledge of the assailant. But for right now, he just wanted her safe and sound. He wanted her out of there. They would have to talk to her later.

He notified RJ that they were leaving and for him to take charge of the scene, and he got into his Mercedes and drove her away from there.

When he held her hand, it was shaking.

CHAPTER THIRTY-ONE

They were in bed, with Grant on his back and Marti on her side. With his arm around her, she had her head resting on his shoulder. He wrapped his other arm around her too. "I know it's upsetting. Try to get some sleep."

But Marti was far too distressed. "If that driver had been a stranger, I would be able to deal with it. But it wasn't a stranger, Grant. It was Eric." Her frown of puzzlement was fixed on her face. "He was a really close friend of mine. He was there, right in my backyard, the night Jaleesa . . . The night of that shooting." She still couldn't talk about it without the pain piercing through. "He was the one that was upset about Andy Sloan crashing her party because he knew I didn't want Andy anywhere near me or my daughter. He was my dog. He was my ride or die."

A part of Grant felt a spark of jealousy when she spoke so lovingly about some man. But he quickly dismissed such foolishness because he knew she felt so betrayed by that man. And that man had tried to kill her. "Something apparently changed."

271

"But what? I haven't seen Eric in years. We haven't talked on the phone, there's been no communication between us, there's been nothing. What could have changed?"

"Maybe he didn't like what happened to your daughter and turned on you?"

But she quickly shook her head. "He stuck with me longer than anybody else. Until I wasn't moving on and he couldn't keep singing that same old song with me. I understood when he moved on. Everybody moved on."

"Except you."

"I would have if I could have," Marti said.

Grant exhaled. "Whatever the reason, it's chilling either way because that was the same pickup truck that I saw on the street cameras I reviewed after you had that car crash. The windows were too tinted for us to see who was inside that truck, but it's the same truck."

Marti nodded. "I know it is."

"Which means he was trying to kill, not just tonight, but earlier this week too."

Marti couldn't hardly wrap her brains around it. Here they were thinking it was a local matter.

"Who would know something? Does this Eric have a family?"

It was when Grant said it that Marti

remembered it. She sat up in bed. "LeeAnn. LeeAnn will know."

"Who's LeeAnn?"

"His wife. She'll know everything." Then she looked at Grant. "I've got to go to Memphis."

Grant stared at her for several seconds. "Are you sure you can handle that, babe?"

Marti's face became even more distressed at the thought of returning to the scene of the crime, as she saw it. Then she exhaled and nodded her head. "I have to. I've got to find out what became of Eric and why he turned our friendship into this level of hate."

She could tell Grant didn't want her to leave Belgrave. He knew Belgrave. He didn't know shit about Memphis. But then he nodded his head. "Looks like we're going to Memphis then," he said.

When he said *we*, Marti's heart soared. "You're going with me?"

"Of course I am! Think I'm going to let you deal with this shit alone? Not on your life, kiddo."

Marti smiled and laid her head, once again, on his shoulder. He held her once again.

At a time like this, she craved his embrace.

CHAPTER THIRTY-TWO

They arrived at the Memphis airport just after eleven that next morning. Grant told RJ that he wouldn't be in that day and neither would Marti. RJ, who loved being in charge, insisted they take all the time they needed, and that he understood their need to regroup after such a harrowing night. He had no idea they weren't even in the state of Florida anymore.

After picking up a rental car, Marti drove

them straight to Eric Peterson's house. But because Eric lived in the same neighborhood she once lived in, to get to his house she had to drive past her house. Or, more correctly, the house she once owned. That was how she and Eric met: He was in the neighborhood walking his dog and she was in the neighborhood walking herself. She and her husband Roger, and Eric and his wife LeeAnn, became fast friends.

When she stopped the car in front of the home she thought was going to be her forever home, Grant knew what that meant.

It was a beautiful mid-century-modern home, he thought, and whoever had purchased it had little kids' toys strewn all over the front lawn.

"I hope they're happy there," Marti said, looking at those toys. "I know I was." Then she squinted her eyes and corrected herself. "Before that night, I was."

Grant took her hand and squeezed it. "You'll be happy again, Markita. I promise you that."

Marti smiled, but she kept her eyes on that house for several more minutes. Then she looked at him. "It's stressful right now, but you have made me happy already, Grant. I didn't think it was possible, but you have."

Grant smiled, leaned over and kissed her, and it was enough. She realized that being in the present with him was enough to lift her beyond her past pain and give her hope for her future. It was time to move on. She removed her feet off of the brake, and moved on.

There were many cars at the Petersons' house when they drove up, as if LeeAnn had already been notified of her husband's demise and family and friends were gathering, so Marti knew she had to tread lightly.

She looked at Grant. Both of them were casually dressed, although he wore a blazer with his jeans and tucked-in shirt and she wore a waist high jacket with her jeans and tucked-in blouse, but there was something about Grant that exuded authority without him even trying to exude it. He had a look, *and skin color*, that Marti knew LeeAnn, an unabashed civil rights activist who blamed *the man* for everything wrong in black people's lives, might not be open to. But she needed him by her side.

"If you don't get a very warm welcome, don't take it personally. LeeAnn is suspicious of white people, I'll just be frank with you. But she means no harm."

"A racist who means no harm," said

Grant. "Got it."

Marti could have argued with him about the definition of racism, but she didn't go there. She wasn't in Memphis to discuss race. She was in Memphis to find out why a brother tried to kill a sister. Period. Full stop.

When she and Grant got out and rang the bell, Marti was surprised to see LeeAnn Peterson answer the door. She could tell she had been crying, but she still looked radiant. But as soon as LeeAnn saw who was standing at her door, it did her in. She pulled her old friend into her arms. "*Oh Marti*!" The two friends hugged and cried. "*Oh Marti*."

For several seconds they hugged each other. And when they pulled back, both women were still emotional. "Come on in," LeeAnn said.

Grant wasn't sure if she even saw him standing beside Marti and he didn't care. He wasn't leaving Marti out of his sight. He kept his arm on her lower back and followed her in.

There was a group of people in the living room, all still digesting the news from what Grant could see, and LeeAnn escorted him and Marti into the kitchen away from the prying eyes. And ears. They sat at the small kitchen table.

"It's so good to see you again," LeeAnn

said to Marti. "I just wish it wasn't under these circumstances."

"Me too, girl. Me too."

But when Marti noticed that LeeAnn was now staring at Grant, she quickly introduced him. "This is Grant McGraw, LeeAnn."

Grant extended his hand. "I'm sorry about your loss, Mrs. Peterson."

She shook his hand. "Thank you."

She was tight-lipped and not nearly as warm toward Grant as she was toward Marti, but he didn't mind. She was cordial. She was civil. She was allowing him to remain in her house and, by extension, by Marti's side. That was enough for him.

"When were you notified?" Marti asked her.

"Late last night. But when they said he was in Belgrave, I thought they said Belfast and I'm like what was he doing in Ireland?"

The two ladies laughed through their tears. "I never heard of no Belgrave, Florida."

"Neither had I," Marti said, "until I was assigned there. By the way, Grant is the chief of police in Belgrave."

"Oh! I don't know why I assumed he was your husband or boyfriend or somebody like that. The way he kept his arm around you and seemed so protective of you."

Marti smiled. "He's also my boyfriend," she said.

LeeAnn laughed. "I knew I wasn't imagining things," she said.

But Marti was confused. "You seem to be taking Eric's death pretty well."

"Oh I cried all night long, girl. I'm nearly out of tears, I cried so long. I took it real hard."

Marti knew it was going to be a tough subject to broach. "I don't know if the caller told you about *how* he died?"

"That's the crazy part," LeeAnn said. "When they said he tried to kill you, I was floored. I'm like *what*? *Eric*? He loved you. I used to think he wanted to be with you more than he wanted me."

That piqued Grant's interest. "You think that could have been his motive?"

But Marti shot that right down. "No way," she said. "He knew I thought of him as a big brother. I could never see him any other way."

Grant didn't like the way she was so dismissive of what he saw as a reasonable motive. "But could he have seen it another way?" he asked the widow.

"I'm with Marti on that one," said LeeAnn. "He might have wanted her, but he knew she didn't want him. Not like that."

"But I still can't figure out why he would do such a crazy thing, Lee," said Marti, her face anguished. "I can't figure out why."

But when LeeAnn said, "I can," both Marti and Grant looked at each other, and then stared at LeeAnn. "You know why?" Marti asked her.

"It's that woman. That's why." Then LeeAnn took a deep breath. "Let me back up. You may not know this, but Eric left me for another woman."

Marti's mouth literally flew open in shock. "He left you?"

"Oh yes. And she had him so wrapped around her finger that he did time for that bitch."

Grant was intrigued. Who was this woman? But Marti was floored. "Eric went to prison?"

"He sure did. Spent almost two years in prison behind her mess."

"Do I know her?"

"Do you know her?" LeeAnn answered Marti's question with a question. Only her question was rhetorical because she quickly answered it herself. "Yes you know her. She was your best friend."

"My best friend?" Then Marti's eyes stretched wider. "Kamille? You mean

280

Kamille? Are you telling me Eric left you to be with *Kamille*?"

"That's absolutely what I'm telling you."

"But they couldn't stand each other!"

"That was the public them. The private them had been having an affair for nearly a year before you left Memphis."

Grant looked at Marti. He could tell she was stunned.

"But you know the crazy part?" LeeAnn said.

"That's not the crazy part?" Marti asked her.

"Even after I found out about the affair," said LeeAnn, "I stayed with his butt. But then, just a few months later, he left me for her anyway. And that's when he got into all that trouble."

"What trouble?"

"Kamille got fired from the police force because she was falsifying records and taking bribes all over the city."

"*Kamille*?" Marti was still flabbergasted. "Kamille was on the take?"

"But guess who was her strongman? Guess what fool was collecting all those bribes for her?"

"Eric? Meek and mild accountant Eric?"

"That's right! His meek and mildness

281

left as soon as he got a taste of Kamille. And he never looked back."

"Okay, this is a lot to unpack here, Lee. This a lot you telling me. So are saying Eric went to prison, but Kamille didn't?"

"That's exactly what I'm saying. She was fired, but she batted her pretty little eyes and they let that heifer slide. But he got two years behind that mess because he was the face of her crimes. He was the collector of her bribes. But if you ask me, it was because he wasn't pretty like her. He wasn't sleeping with all them rich, white men downtown who could say the word and get him off scot-free like they got her off." She said that and glanced at Grant, as if he had something to do with it.

But Grant was worried about Marti's mental health. He could tell she was so overwhelmed with the news that she was checking out. She couldn't. She just couldn't anymore.

That was when he took over. "You said you're convinced he tried to murder Markita because of her best friend Kamille. But why would Kamille want her best friend dead?"

Marti looked at LeeAnn too. It was a reasonable question.

"I can't tell you Kamille's motivations. I don't know that woman anymore. I never thought she'd sleep with my husband, but she did to the point of him leaving me for her. But I know this: Every bad thing that Eric got involved with involved her. Even when he got out of prison, he went straight back to her."

"She took him back?"

"Oh yeah. She ain't giving up a flunky like him. Gave him a job in her restaurant and everything. But you know that old saying that if you find a willing horse you ride it? She was gon' ride that willing horse until it fell." Then LeeAnn exhaled. "It fell last night."

But Marti heard something else. "What restaurant?"

"I keep forgetting you haven't been around here in years. But yeah, after she was fired from the force, she opened up her own restaurant with all that money from all her sugar daddies. And it's been doing surprisingly well. One of the most successful in town."

Grant looked at Marti. Marti couldn't do anything but shake her head. Kamille a restaurateur? *Kamille*? But then again, she would never have believed Kamille would sleep with her friend's husband or be on the take. It was a lot she didn't know about her so-called best friend.

"Do you know where she lives?" Grant asked LeeAnn.

"No. But she's always at that restaurant. I know where that is."

"Give us the address," Grant said as he stood up. They needed to get on with it.

After giving him the address, both women hugged it out again, said their goodbyes, and then Marti and Grant left.

Marti was still reeling from all that news and wanted to stay and comfort her friend, but she knew Grant was right. They needed to get on with it. They needed answers.

CHAPTER THIRTY-THREE

Although Grant cautioned Marti against taking the word of a scorned widow regarding her best friend's involvement with what Eric was up to, Marti knew LeeAnn too well. She was loud and proud. She was narrow-minded and quick to blame race for everything. But she was no drama queen. She was no liar. You could take what LeeAnn said to the bank.

But then again, she thought, she'd always believed that about Kamille and Eric too!

"I'll take what you said under advisement," was all she said to Grant after he gave her his caution.

That was why Grant got Marti to contact a couple cops she trusted at the Memphis PD and invite them along in case an arrest needed to be made.

The two cops, both detectives who still had a fondness for their former boss, hugged Marti when they met up in the restaurant's parking lot.

"We'll be around back," said the senior detective, "in case she tries to make a run for it."

"And we'll cover the front," said Grant, and the foursome split up.

Marti was impressed by the beauty of the building and the fact that the parking lot was nearly filled with cars. It was lunch time and apparently they had a large lunch crowd.

But Marti wasn't surprised. "If Kamille was going to do it," she said, "it was going to be big and bold. That's her," she added as she and Grant made their way toward the front entrance. "That's her."

But when they got inside, it was so filled with customers that they had to search and search before they found her. They didn't want to ask anybody if they knew where she was because she might have refused to see them and took off.

"There she is," Marti said when she finally spotted her.

Grant looked where she was nodding. When he saw a beautiful black woman standing at a table seemingly thanking some of her customers, he could easily see how that lady and Marti would have been besties. They looked so much alike to him. Not like twins, but certainly like sisters. He almost had to do a double take.

"Come on," Marti said as she and Grant made their way toward the back part of the huge restaurant where Kamille Oliver was standing. They were almost there when Kamille started laughing at something somebody at that table said and looked over her restaurant. That was when she saw them approaching. Her eyes locked in with Marti's eyes, and the terror in Kamille's eyes told the story.

For Grant, he saw a woman who never thought in a million years Marti would have put two and two together and found her best friend at the end of the chain of events that should have led to Marti's death.

For Marti, she saw shame and regret and sadness in Kamille's eyes, as if her true colors were coming out and she wanted them back in. But it was too late.

And Kamille took off running toward the back of the restaurant.

Marti and Grant ran after her. There was no way she was getting away with this! They toppled one waiter with his tray of food, another waiter with his tray of glasses, as they ran after Kamille.

Kamille ran through her kitchen and then out of the back door where, they would later find out, her Bentley was parked.

But as soon as she ran out of her back door and made her way down her backsteps, the two detectives, one on each side of the building, yelled for her to stop.

By the time Marti and Grant ran outside, Kamille had stopped running and had placed her hands in the air, her back to every one of them. Marti and Grant hurried down the backsteps.

"Now turn around!" yelled one of the detectives, their guns trained on Kamille as if she was some common criminal, not the successful businesswoman she had remade herself into being.

But as Kamille was turning around, Marti knew her friend too well. She was packing and she was pulling it out. And Marti panicked. "Kamille *don't*!" she yelled to warn her friend.

But Kamille was already turning around with two Glocks already pulled out of her pockets, and both of them firing at the cops.

She shot one detective, but the other one shot her. Repeatedly.

Marti was devastated. "Stop shooting!" Grant yelled at the second detective as he and Marti ran to her friend.

But when she got there and cradled Kamille's head on her lap, Kamille was barely breathing.

"Why Millie?" a stricken Marti asked her friend. "Why?"

288

But before Kamille could say the word she was struggling to say, she was shot again.

Grant and Marti jumped up and looked. The second detective, the one that had taken her down to begin with, looked pale. "She was reaching for her gun!" he yelled. "She was reaching for her gun!"

Grant and Marti looked at each other. They didn't see her reaching for anything! But Grant stopped Marti from pointing that out. He didn't know this town. He didn't know who they could trust in this town. Kamille was a dead woman anyway. It was doubtful if she had the strength to breathe another breath, let alone tell them anything. He wanted to get his lady out of this town and get her out alive. He stopped her from saying a word.

CHAPTER THIRTY-FOUR

They decided to tell the Police as little as possible. They didn't even mention LeeAnn. And because they had nothing to hold them on, and since neither of them had even drawn their weapons, they were allowed to leave.

Marti wanted to stay longer, to see if she could get more answers, but Grant wanted her out of Memphis. That detective, a man Marti had trusted, wanted to silence Kamille. That cockamamie story about her reaching for her gun was bullshit and they both knew it. But why did he want to silence her all of a sudden? If it wasn't related to Marti, then why would they wait until Marti was in town to silence her?

No way was Grant allowing her to remain another hour in that town. They took the next flight back home.

But when they arrived in town that night and Grant was driving them home, he was still holding her hand as Marti was still digesting it all. Until she said something that caught Grant's full attention. "She was such a good friend to me. Had it not been for her, I wouldn't have even had this job. She got me this job."

Grant looked at her. "Kamille got you the consultant's job?"

Marti nodded. "Yeah, she did. She knew I was running out of my savings fast and was struggling to make ends meet. I was thinking about working at McDonald's just to get some income. That's when she told me to go to Florida, that the Assistant AG's office was hiring a slew of police consultants to help them clean up some bad police departments in their state. She said the pay was lousy, and most of the people they hired were kids straight out of college looking for a temp gig until their real jobs came through, but she said with my police background I could do that job with my eyes closed. And I agreed with her. And since I was looking to leave Missouri, because that's where I was at the time, I decided to apply. And I got approved right away."

"And you assumed that was because of your extensive police background," said Grant.

Marti nodded. "Why wouldn't I assume that?"

"It never occurred to you, because it sure as hell occurred to me as soon as I saw your credentials, that you were super-duper overly qualified for the position?"

Marti thought about it. Then she had to agree with Grant. "I knew I was overly qualified, but I was in a place where I was barely able to get out of bed. I had been going from state to state and town to town in those different states. I was eyeing McDonald's when Kamille phoned me, that's the kind of shape I was in. I needed help, and she knew it."

"And maybe she exploited it to her end," said Grant.

Marti looked at him. She knew she had blinders on when it came to her friends in Memphis, just like Grant had blinders on when it came to his peeps in Belgrave. But just like she was able to show him the way in Belgrave, she knew he could show her the way regarding her Memphis connections. "How did she exploit me?" she asked because she wasn't connecting the dots.

"She tells you about this lowly job in Florida. You get the job easily when most employers would declare you were too qualified and therefore conclude you wouldn't be a good employee. They wouldn't want to touch that. But they hired you lickety-split."

"Okay I'm following you there. But I still don't see how me getting this job helps Kamille."

"Think about it, Marti. You get the job. Your first assignment is in Belgrave. On the very day you show up, and I mean within minutes of your arrival, Belgrave suffers its first mass casualty event in the history of the town. The very first one on your very first day."

Marti continued to stare at him. "Go on."

"Then, in that same week, we suffer our second mass casualty event in history! That's a hell of a coincidence."

Marti couldn't help but agree with that. "But I'm still not seeing how this helps Kamille."

Grant ran his hand across his tired face. "I don't see it yet, either, but there has to be one. Because then, a month later, Eric Peterson shows up, your friend and Kamille's flunky boyfriend. And he tries to kill you twice." Grant shook his head. "Something stinks in Denmark. We just have to figure out why."

Marti leaned her head back. "What's going on?" she asked with anguish in her voice. But she didn't ask it so that he could answer her because she knew he couldn't, but so that she could verbalize her own internal frustration. And her own dread that whoever was behind all of this was relentless. And that they weren't going to quit until she was sleeping in her grave. In Belgrave.

Marti was scared.

Until Grant realized something. "Wait a minute," he said and Marti looked up at him. "Wait a minute," he said again.

"What is it, Grant?"

It looked as if Grant's mind was searching through his rolodex of information and was trying to pull something out. "Is it a K or a C?"

"Is what a K or a C?"

"Kamille. How does she spell her name?"

"It's Kamille Oliver with a K."

Oliver, he thought. "I remember."

"You remember what?"

"I remember that name."

"What name? Eric's name?"

"No. Kamille's. I saw that name."

Marti was suddenly hopeful. "Where?"

And Grant suddenly realized where. He quickly looked in his rearview and then made a quick U-turn.

"Where are we going?" Marti asked him. "Back to Memphis?"

"No," he said. "To the police station."

Marti didn't know why, but Grant seemed to know exactly why. She was willing to let him continue to work it out internally and she'd find out once he had.

She leaned back and remained silent.

And hopeful.

CHAPTER THIRTY-FIVE

RJ and Pete were in Pete's office with Samuel Feltz, the commanding officer the AG's office sent to Belgrave to clean up the department.

"It's needed," RJ said. "There's no doubt about that. But let me be clear," he added to the man seated next to him. They were in Pete's office seated in front of Pete's desk. "I love Grant McGraw. I am not his enemy. He's a good man."

Feltz stared at Captain Jeffers, the man who had the most to gain if McGraw was booted out. "But?"

"He's a businessman," RJ said. "He's not a cop. He's not a chief."

"This department has gone to hell in a handbasket under his leadership," said Pete. "Chief has to go. Bottom line."

"I see he has very loyal men working for him," Feltz said.

RJ and Pete looked at each other. They realized they were showing their hand.

"All we're saying," said RJ, "is that we need new leadership."

"We desperately need new leadership,"

added Pete.

"I hear you, but not so fast guys," Feltz said. "No decisions have been made about who stays or who goes. I just got here."

"There he is," RJ said and they all looked out of the window too. Grant's Mercedes had just driven up. Grant got out and opened the passenger door for Marti.

"He's sleeping with her you know," Pete said as the couple began heading for the entrance.

Feltz was surprised. "Is he?"

"They live together," RJ added. "You didn't know that, did you?"

Feltz exhaled. "No, I did not."

But when Grant and Marti entered the building, Pete called out from his office. "Chief? *Chief*?"

But Grant and Marti ignored his calls and kept on walking.

"The guy from Tallahassee is here!" Pete yelled out again, but that didn't stop them either. Because Grant was singularly focused. They went into Grant's office.

While Marti closed *and locked* the door behind them, Grant hurried behind his desk and turned on his computer. Then he looked up the background intel they had on the Wafer House shooter.

"There it is!" Grant said after strolling down. "I knew I saw that name before. I remembered it because it was spelled with a K."

Marti was leaned against him, looking at the computer screen too. "Kamille's name is in this report?"

"The Wafer House shooter was married three times. Look," he said. "His second wife was a Kamille Oliver."

When he said that name, Marti leaned in closer. And she saw Kamille's name. "She was married to the Wafer House shooter?"

"Yes! It didn't last long, probably because she had moved on to some other sucker, but there's the connection. She used him like she used Eric Peterson."

"But to what end?" asked Marti.

Grant leaned back. "That's the part I don't know."

"What about the two shooters at Karney's grocery store? Is there a connection there?"

Grant leaned forward again and searched his computer for the background they had on the two Karney's grocery store shooters. On the first shooter, he found no connection whatsoever. "Nothing on the first one," he said, and began looking at the second one.

"Which one is which?" asked Marti.

"The one I'm looking at now is the one we surrounded in his trailer."

"The one your own officer shot and killed because he claimed he had spit on him and head-butted him when there was absolutely no evidence of that?"

Grant nodded. "That's the one." And then his eyes lit up. "And there *is* a connection!" he declared.

"What is it?"

"He was born and raised in Memphis," Grant said.

"That's a connection," said Marti, "but it's kind of weak."

But Grant found something else. "He also spent time in prison there."

"At the same time Eric was there?"

"I don't know when Eric was imprisoned."

But then Grant saw a single sentence on his rap sheet that caught his eye. "While incarcerated, the shooter was accused of shanking another prisoner, but his cellmate testified that he was in his cell the entire time. "His cellmate," Grant said, looking up at Marti, "was Eric Peterson."

Marti was floored. "They were

cellmates?"

Grant nodded. "Yes." Then he smiled. "Still think it's weak?"

She shook her head. "Hell nall."

"And if that's not enough, guess where the shooter's last known employment was?"

"Kamille's restaurant?"

"He worked at Kamille's restaurant, yes, ma'am."

Marti couldn't believe it. "They both link back to Kamille."

"Right. Like they were puppets on her string. And I saw that woman with my own two eyes," Grant added. "She's stunning. I could see men falling for her like that. Easily."

"And I can see her using men like that," Marti hated to admit it. "Easily. But I still don't understand why she would go after me. Because those mass shooters wouldn't hurt me by shooting up a lot of people. But they would discredit you."

"Right," said Grant.

"But then are you the target," asked Marti, "or am I?"

"Or," said Grant, "are both of us?"

"But *why*?" Marti was distressed.

"You said she phoned you and told you to apply for the job. You weren't even living in Florida at the time."

"No, I wasn't. But she knew I was moving all over the place."

"Did she give you a name to contact?"

"Yes. She told me to call the Assistant Attorney General directly, to say her name, and he would hire me. And he did."

"Over the phone?"

"Based on Kamille's recommendation, yes."

"So the mayor might be right."

"About what?"

"The governor is trying to discredit him because he knows Dooney is planning to run for governor himself in the upcoming election."

"But I thought Governor Devere was under term limits and couldn't run again."

"He can't. But his handpicked successor, Jake Crocker, the Assistant Attorney General, can. And he intends to do so. And Mayor Dooney Rickter will easily be his toughest opponent."

And that was when it all came together for Grant. "That's it!" he said out loud.

"What's it?" asked Marti.

"Why didn't I think of that before!"

"Think of what before?"

But Grant turned off his computer and was on his feet again. He grabbed Marti's hand and they hurried out of his office.

But as soon as they neared the exit, Commander Feltz was hurrying out of Pete's office. "Sir, I need to talk to you," he said to Grant as he hurried behind him. "Sir, I'm with the Attorney General's office. Sir?"

When he exited the building and hurried down the steps behind Grant and Marti, he continued to call out Grant's name.

Grant knew he couldn't hide from him forever. "Hop in," he said to Feltz as he opened the door for Marti and then hurried around to the driver side door. Commander Feltz, seizing the opportunity, hopped into the backseat.

"Where are we going?" the commander asked Grant.

"Who are you again?" Grant asked him, looking through his rearview mirror.

"I'm Commander Feltz. I was assigned to check out this department."

"Assigned by who? Jake Crocker?"

"The Assistant Attorney General, yes sir. Now is that enough backstory for you to answer my question and tell me where we're going?"

"That's enough backstory for me not to tell you anything," Grant responded, and sped even faster.

Marti was as in the dark as the

commander was, but like before, she was willing to let Grant work it out in his head rather than pepper him with questions. But when they were pulling up to a condominium building, she was too curious. "Who lives here?" she asked him.

But before he could answer, she saw who. Celeste. His former plaything. She was coming out of the front of the building.

Grant got out and hurried toward her as she made her way to her car the valet had just drove around. Marti and Commander Feltz got out and hurried behind Grant.

"What's this about, Chief McGraw?" Feltz hurried up to Grant and asked him.

"She's his niece."

"She's whose niece?"

"Jake Crocker."

Marti and Feltz were both surprised.

"That woman," Grant said as they hurried toward Celeste, "is the Assistant AG's niece. She's your boss's niece."

"That's very interesting," said Feltz as they hurried, "I'll give you that. But why should it be dispositive?"

"Because of Marti's angle in this."

"What do you mean my angle in it?" Marti was struggling to keep up with the two men.

"When I said we both might be the targets, I was right," said Grant. "But we're the targets for different reasons."

"Why was I the target?"

"You're by the book and Kamille knew it," said Grant. "You wouldn't hold back in your reports of how awful a police department we were. But they didn't plan on anything else happening."

"What else happened?" Marti was still puzzled. But then they were upon Celeste just as she was opening her car door.

"Celeste!" Grant called out.

Standing between her car's opened door and front seat, she turned around when she heard Grant's voice. And immediately Marti saw the fear in her eyes when she saw he was not alone. "What are you doing here?" she asked, looking at Marti and Feltz more than she was looking at Grant.

"The game is up, Celeste," Grant said. "I know why you did it. I know you got your uncle to handle it because the person he assigned to come here was by the book. She'd discredit the mayor just by doing her job. He knew, through Kamille, that Marti couldn't be bought. And you knew all about it because you and Uncle Jake are tight. But then something happened that threw a wrench in it for you."

Celeste was now staring at Grant. "What happened?"

"Instead of you getting me to fall in love with you," Grant said, "I fell in love with the very woman that was supposed to bring the mayor down and, by association, bring me down right along with him."

"That's absurd. Why would I go along with somebody bringing you down, if I loved you so much as you claim?"

It was a good question to Marti and Feltz too. They both looked at Grant.

"Because a weakened man," said Grant, "is a needy man. I would be right where you wanted me to be: ripe and ready for a barracuda like you to swallow whole."

Grant hit the nail on the head because Celeste suddenly looked different to Marti. She suddenly looked wounded the way she did when she was arguing with Grant in his office. "You chose her over me," she said, "when I told you I was willing to leave my husband for you."

"And I told you that you and I were never going to be anything more than what we were, and you knew that from the start," said Grant.

"But I loved you! You just met her. How

305

could you choose her over me?"

But Grant didn't want to hear that wang about love. "Did you ask Jake Crocker to get Eric Peterson to kill Marti?" he asked her, getting on with it.

"I don't know who he got, but I told him she was ruining everything for me. I told him how you let her stay all night with you when you would never even let me visit your house! He hired her because he knew she was by the book like you said and she would write a terrible report about the police department that would discredit the mayor when he runs for governor. But I told him she was in love with you and you were in love with her and she would never again write any more bad reports after that first one. She would probably rescind that first report and claim she didn't even write it to protect you. I told him he didn't need her anymore. And he agreed," Celeste said.

Marti never believed in grand conspiracies. Until now. "Who's Kamille Oliver to your uncle?" she asked.

"She's a hoe, if you ask me, but she's his girlfriend. She wants to be first lady of Florida some day when Uncle Jake runs for governor and wins. He told her whatever he wanted and she went out and found the people to do the job. She found you. She found Eric.

She found RJ and Pete Kerrigan on the local level to make sure everything stayed on track. But you had to fall in love with Grant," she said with tears welling up in her eyes. "And he fell in love with you."

Then before they realized it, she had pulled a gun out of her pocket with her car door giving her cover. And before anybody could respond, she pointed it directly at Grant's head.

"Whoa," said Feltz, backing up, his hands in the air.

"I'll kill him if anybody makes a move. I'll kill him!"

"I'll leave town," Marti said, begging her. "Please don't shoot. I'll leave right now and never come back. You can have him!"

But Celeste wasn't buying it. "You liar," she said. "Nobody can be with Grant and give him up. Nobody!" she screamed, and then she fired her weapon, causing Marti to scream even louder.

But Grant had moved his body before she fired that shot, but not enough. Although he wasn't shot in the head where she was aiming, he was shot in the arm as he was turning away from her. He fell to the ground and Marti fell to the ground with him.

Celeste pointed her gun at Feltz before hopping in her car and trying to drive away.

But Feltz pulled out his Magnum and began running with the car. "Stop now or I'll shoot!" he yelled as he ran. "Stop or I'll shoot! Stop!"

When she still would not stop, Feltz let it rip. He fired and fired. He nearly emptied his chambers firing on Celeste.

Apparently one or more of those bullets took her out because the car suddenly began to drift, and then it slowed, and then it finally came to a stop.

Marti was helping Grant on his feet when the car came to a stop. "I'm alright," Grant was saying to Marti as he held onto his wounded arm and they both ran over to where the car had stopped.

When they got there, Feltz was forcing open the jammed car door. When he opened it, they all could see that Celeste was hunched over the steering wheel and definitely dead.

"I know you don't believe me," Feltz said, "but I had nothing to do with this madness. I had no idea any of that was going on."

Grant was staring at Celeste. "I know you didn't," he said.

Feltz looked at him. "When did you know that?"

"When you were willing to shoot to kill

your boss's niece," Grant said, and looked at the commander. "I knew it then."

Feltz nodded his head. "And don't you worry. I'm turning this case over to the FBI right now. And everybody involved, from the local cops to anybody in the governor's administration, including my boss, will be prosecuted to the fullest extent of the law. I promise you that." He looked at Marti. "Both of you."

Marti smiled. Grant nodded. "Thank you," he said as they could hear sirens in the distance.

Marti placed her arm around Grant's waist. "You need to sit down," she said, "so I can stop your bleeding."

He looked at her with a sincerity that warmed her heart. "You already have," he said to her. "You already have."

COMING OUT OF THE COLD

EPILOGUE

Grant McGraw was alone.

His back against the wall, he was in agony. One year ago, his life completely changed. One year ago, he was having nightmares and cold sweats and terrible sleepless nights.

But now, he felt even more alone.

On the positive side, if he could even think of one, he managed to clean up his department. Before the FBI even arrived, Grant fired and then arrested RJ, Pete, and Carter, and the cop that shot the gunman that was holed up in that trailer. He got rid of all the bad apples in his department, and the FBI did the rest. Everybody involved, top to bottom, was being prosecuted. That was a big positive.

But on the negative side were days like this.

"Chief McGraw?"

He looked as if he was expecting horrific news. That was why he couldn't even respond to the man.

"Sir, you can go in now."

Grant exhaled. And steeled himself.

And took what felt like the longest walk of his life down that winding corridor. His heart was hammering. His breathing was staggered. He walked like a wino. Because he was absolutely expecting the worst.

When he got to the door, he couldn't take it anymore. He turned around and grabbed the man by his coat lapel. "You have to tell me now," he said. "You have to tell me! Did one of them survive? Or neither?"

When the man smiled, Grant wanted to punch his lights out. What on earth was funny? He was dying over here and this fool was *smiling*?

"Go on in, sir."

Grant hesitated again. But he knew he was going to have a heart attack if he didn't face it and face it head on.

He flung open that door and went inside.

And there she was. Which caused his heartbeat to stop pounding. She was alive!

But she was sitting up in bed, which confused him. How could she be sitting up after all she went through? But there she was. And she wasn't crying. She wasn't stricken with grief. She was smiling too!

And she held their precious brand-new baby girl in her arms.

"Come and see her, Grant," Marti said

with tears of joy in her eyes. "Come and see her."

Grant walked like he was walking on glue. It took him forever. But when he got there and saw that gorgeous little brown bombshell of a baby staring her huge eyes up at him, he nearly buckled.

"Take her," Marti said. "She bites, but she won't bite you. She doesn't have the teeth for it."

Marti laughed, but Grant couldn't even break a smile.

He looked at Marti. She was the chief trainer for the Belgrave Police Department and the chairman of the Belgrave Oversight Board. She was now the head of the BOBs. That was how remarkable the town embraced her. That was how remarkable Grant knew, from the moment he met her, she was. "The doctor said you and the baby were in grave distress. The doctor said you or the baby or both of you might not make it. You made it?"

Marti laughed. "You ask as if it's a question whether I did or not." But her smile left when she saw how distressed *he* was. "Yes, darling," she said, "I made it. The baby made it too."

And it was only after she said it did Grant believe it. And he took his baby girl from the arms of his wife and placed her in his arms. He smiled as soon as he saw her scrunch up her tiny little face. "Yep," he said with a huge grin. "She's a worrier. She's ours." And both of them laughed, causing the baby to grin too.

And in that instant, just holding their little girl, Grant McGraw fell in love for only the second time in his entire life.

His wife and his brand-new daughter, he decided in that moment, were the loves of his life.

Visit
mallorymonroe.com
or
austinbrookpublishing.com
or
amazon.com/author/mallorymonroe
for more information on all of her one-hundred-and-fifty-plus books.

ABOUT THE AUTHOR

Mallory Monroe is the author of over one-hundred-and-fifty bestselling novels.

Visit
mallorymonroebooks.com
or
austinbrookpublishing.com
or
amazon.com/author/mallorymonroe

for more information on all her titles.

Made in the USA
Middletown, DE
06 March 2025

72324532R00182